This is dedicated to anyone who has loved someone so much it hurt. No relationship is perfect, but you can make the relationship you have perfect for you.

Love, humor, and forgiveness, are nothing without communication and trust

Straight Up

Merci Crandall

Merci is heartbroken but determined to forget about Ryan after learning that he and his wife are expecting their first child.

She has a fantastic new job as the personal assistant to the partner of one of the most prestigious law firms in the state. She's an independent woman for the first time in her life, and everything is almost perfect.

If she could just forget about the man, who changed everything for her. Only he keeps popping up in the most unexpected places…

Ryan West

Ryan was determined to make his marriage work once he found out he and his wife were expecting. He wants his child to feel loved and wanted after knowing for himself what it felt like for a child who was just a means to an end.

He once loved Tricia, and he knew they would have to work hard on their relationship. So, he arranged for her to come with him to one of his resorts in the Caribbean; it was going to be a working vacation.

He would leave all thoughts of Merci behind. But try as hard as he could, he still couldn't get her out of his mind. Everywhere he looked, he could still picture her face and hear her whimsical laughter. Was it just his imagination…?

Chapter One

Ryan

I was patiently waiting to hear the news from Tricia's doctor. I couldn't believe it when she first told me. I was finally going to be a father. We were going to have a baby, so I'd started focusing on getting our lives back together. I did love Tricia still, but the thoughts of Merci, and wondering about her often crossed my mind. I hoped that whatever she had decided to do with her life would work out for her.

My cell phone rang, and I picked it up. "Hello, Tricia. What did the doctor say? I wish you had let me take you there this morning? How far along are you? When will he run that test? Tricia, I'm glad we decided to try again. Having a child in our lives will be the best thing for us and our marriage. I will see you soon. Yes, and I love you!"

My phone rang again; it was Zane. I silenced the call; I didn't want to explain anything to him just yet. It rang again, and knowing him as well as I did, he wouldn't keep calling unless it was something important.

"Zane, why are you blowing up my phone? What did you say? Are you sure it was her?" I listened while he told me about running into Merci earlier that morning. She was on the way to work and had happened to be at the coffee shop he frequented in downtown Seattle.

"Did you get a chance to speak with her?" We talked for a few more minutes. I desperately wanted to get more information about

Merci from him, but it was best if I didn't know any of the details. He started to tell me which coffee shop it was, and I interrupted him by mentioning the baby.

"Are you at the gym? I'll talk to you then." I grabbed my stuff and headed outside and climbed into my Jag.

~

"Congrats, buddy. Are you sure this is what you want?" Zane didn't seem convinced.

"What do you mean by that, You, know how much I wanted a child of my own. It's just taken us a little longer to get her pregnant. Spot me. So, would you?"

Zane moved around to stand behind me. "Would I what? So… things are getting better at home then?"

"Wouldn't you want a child of your own? Someone to carry on your name and hang out with you. You can lower the bar. Just come on out and say it, Zane. Quit pussy footing around and ask me. It doesn't mean that I'm going to answer, but you can try."

"You guys having sex regularly now? I mean like happily ever after couples do?" Zane asked me as he stared down at my face.

"Ten more, then we can switch. Nobody has marriages like that nowadays. There's too much life going on out there. Don't look at me like that. We had sex that weekend a few other times. It was almost like the good old days. Help me get up; then we can switch off."

Zane laid down on the bench, and I pulled off most of the weights before I lowered the bar. "Hilarious, Ryan. You are quite the comedian."

After Zane made that remark, I thought about the last things that Merci had said to me. 'So now you're a mind reader and a magician?' I shook the memory from my thoughts.

"Ryan, add more weights. Don't be such a dick!"

"Right. Let me know when to stop."

We went into the sauna after our workout and sat there for a while. I looked over at my friend. "You've lost a lot of weight lately. Nice! What have you been doing differently?"

Zane flexed for me then laughed. "I decided it was time to look for Miss right. That's all it took. I've been careful, and I'm talking meticulous about what I eat. I cut out most of the carbs, and I have lots of protein and veggies. Good ones. That reminds me, do you want to go to the club this weekend?"

"Your mind works in mysterious ways. Sorry, I can't. Tricia and I are going to take a trip to the island before she gets too far along in the pregnancy. She wants to be able to wear her bikini while we are there. I'm exploring my property while we're there to see if I can expand it. Besides, I promised her that I would only go out if she were with me."

He threw back his head and laughed out loud. "She's got you whipped! Yep, you're a goner, Ryan. I hope it works out for you, Pal. I really do."

So, did I. "At least I'm going to give it a try. Who knows, maybe we both need a child in our lives to get our marriage back on track."

Merci

I absolutely loved my new job! I felt like I was finally a contributing member of society. I'd never had one before and had taken care of my two girls right from the start of mine and Paul's marriage. That nightmare was finally over, and I was still living with my parents, but I was slowly working towards my independence.

"Merci, is that you? Fancy meeting you here twice in one week. How's the new job coming along?"

I'd been ecstatic when I'd first seen Zane the other day. I'd wanted to ask him all about Ryan, and how he was doing. But I hadn't said a word. He was no longer in my life. He'd made it quite clear who he wanted to be with.

"I love it, Zane. How are you doing? You are looking fantastic. You've been working out, haven't you?"

"You ought to come with me sometime, Merci. Oh, don't get me wrong, you look perfect just the way you are. What I meant to say was it's a fun thing to do with someone else. Working out is what I meant to say. I'd love to show you how to use all the equipment."

I liked Zane. He had been quite charming the night he had been at the club with Ryan and Brock. "That does sound like fun. How often do you go?"

"I've been trying to go more often lately. I usually meet Ryan there twice a week… Whoops, sorry. Maybe it's not a good idea to have you go with me after all. It could be harder for you knowing that Ryan was going to be a father soon."

"Wh…what did you say?" For some reason, I remembered Ryan saying something about waiting for some good news. He must have been waiting to find out whether his wife was expecting. "Tell him congratulations for me. Listen, Zane. I've got to hurry; I don't want to be late. Maybe I'll see you again here soon."

"Sure, Merci. Later babe!"

I was not his babe, and I'd make every effort that I could to avoid this coffee shop in the future. If Ryan and his wife were going to have a child soon, I didn't want to know about it. I hadn't been aware that I was crying until somebody bumped into me and almost knocked me down. "I'm so sorry; please forgive me. I've got to hurry, or I'll be late for work."

"Miss, are you alright? Did I hurt you?" The man sounded so sincere, and I felt like a ninny when I realized why he had asked me.

"Thank you; I'm fine. I just found out that I've lost someone I loved very much..."

I thanked the gentleman, then rushed past him to get to my building. I would have to hurry now, my makeup would be smeared all over my face, and I wanted to make the right impression when I met the partner of the law firm that I now worked for.

~~

After entering the pristine women's restroom, I set my coffee cup on the counter top, then grabbed a paper towel and wet it to wipe off the mascara tracks on my cheeks.

"Get over him, Merci, he's happy where he is." Eventually, I would be happy too. Now, if I could just convince my inner hooker of that fact, then I could move on. I re-applied my lipstick and pinched my cheeks. Then I made a goofy face at myself and laughed. "Okay, chunky monkey. You've had your cry for the day, now get to work!"

Ryan

I could have kicked myself in the ass for not letting Zane tell me where he had seen Merci. There were at last twenty coffee shops in town where she could have been. Why couldn't I stop obsessing over her? It was best that I forget I'd ever met her and focus on getting mine and Tricia's marriage back on track. We were going to be parents; that thought had made me happier than I thought it would. By this time next year, I would finally be a father.

After I left the gym, I went back to my office in the city to sort through the paperwork that I had started for my property on the island. It needed renovations, and expansion at the same time made sense to me. I'd get all my files together and drop them off at my lawyer's then head home and get ready for the coming vacation.

I was looking forward to having some time off, plus I'd already decided to try and work on our marriage. If we were going to have this child together, we had both better do our best to make it work. I didn't want my child having any doubts that it was wanted. My parents had used me as a pawn my whole youth, and now I hardly spoke to either one of them.

I made a few phone calls to arrange our flight, then I spoke with Jameron Sebastián who was my General manager at The Western Wind which was my Saint Lucia island resort. I let him know that both Tricia and I would be there for a few weeks and maybe longer.

After going through the other monthly reports from the rest of my properties, I was restless. I didn't want to put a name on the reason, but her face still haunted my dreams.

The way I'd left Merci in the parking lot after leading her on and setting her up in her own room had been very wrong. I felt like the biggest kind of jerk. What I had done to her had been unfair both times that I had been with her. Best laid plans hadn't happened for either one of us.

It was too late to cry over spilled milk. I'd made my choice and I needed to stick with it; move on. I had to find a way to keep the memory of Merci from interfering. I knew the first place to start was my decision to take this vacation with Tricia.

Chapter Two

Ryan

A trip to the island with my wife was exactly what I needed. I looked at the time, the morning had dragged by, but I'd accomplished everything that I had set out to do. It was almost one. I decided to call Troy Masters and see if he could fit me in earlier. If not, I might change my appointment for tomorrow. Either that or I'd forgo a visit entirely and fax him the paperwork from Jamaica.

I called Troy's office and was informed by his secretary that he was at a business lunch and he wouldn't be back until later in the afternoon. Well, that made my choice easier. "Could you let Troy know that I will fax him the files from Jamaica? Thank you, Cecilia. Have him call if he needs anything else from me. I will, yes I'm bringing Tricia with me. You have a great afternoon as well, Cecilia. Goodbye."

Now, what do I do with the rest of my afternoon? I guess a drink at the club wouldn't hurt anything. I hadn't been there for at least a month. I knew Jake wouldn't say anything to Tricia if I came in there on my lunch break. He wouldn't anyway; he was loyal to me and the tips I gave him.

I drove to the Surrender and decided to forgo parking with the valet. It was hot outside, and I knew of a perfect place in the shade where I could park my Jag. It was away from the rest of the crowds, and it would be safer from getting any dings or dents parked there.

My cell phone started ringing, and I'd almost didn't answer when I saw who was calling. "Tricia, I was just getting ready to have lunch. Where are you?" I stopped walking and covered my other ear so I could hear her better. The group leaving the club were making quite a ruckus.

I turned around and stepped into the trees, so I could hear what she was saying. "I'm sorry, Tricia. I just can't hear you, the reception in this area isn't any good. I'll call you after I have lunch. Love you too." I was glad she hadn't asked where I was having said lunch. I didn't want to lie to her, so not saying anything at all seemed all right.

I crossed the parking lot just in time to see the man I had tried calling earlier leaving the club. Troy Masters wasn't alone; he had his usual group with him which included Gregory Marx. The others waited at the valet for their cars, and Troy stood there talking with Gregory as I approached. I wondered what he and Marx were up to now. Just before I reached him, I saw a woman step out of the club, and all bets were off. I almost turned around and raced back to my car.

"Ryan, no wonder I can never get ahold of you. Did Cecelia tell you I was here? Oh, have you met Gregory Marx yet?"

He made the introductions, and I did my best to avoid looking at Merci. She was stunning in her pencil thin white skirt and black modest blouse. I supposed that whatever I had done to her had just made her more determined to succeed on her own. She was thin as a rail, and I would never have recognized her as the same woman who I'd first met here months ago. Sophisticated, and self-assured were only a few of the words I thought of to describe her now.

She also made every effort to avoid looking at me. Troy turned to see her walking down the stairs; he hurried over and took her hand to help her down the few remaining steps. Then he led her over to the car while keeping close to her side.

"Hey, West, we need to play a round of golf soon. How's your wife, Patricia doing? How long has it been since you've been to the Western Wind? I know it's a few years or longer since we were there together." Since when did Masters start referring to my wife as Patricia?

That was more information than I wanted Merci to hear. I was still in shock to find her working for my old friend. "I'll play golf with you when you stop cheating. Business lunch?" My eyes darted over toward Merci. What I wanted to do was take her back inside the club and sit down with her and ask her how her life was going. If I'd arrived thirty minutes earlier, I could have invited myself to sit with them and do just that.

"Of course, it was a leisurely one. Are you stopping by the office? We need to update some of your information." I didn't miss the look he gave Merci. "Call Cecelia and make an appointment, better yet just stop by. I will speak to you soon, Mr. Marx." He waited until the gentleman was in his town car, then he clapped me on the shoulder. "We are running late. See you soon, Ryan." Masters possessively placed his hand on Merci's lower back and led her toward his town car.

"Well, you son of a bitch." I continued watching until she was behind the smoky glass windows. I had no longer had the right to care who Merci chose to see, after all, I'd made it clear I didn't want her in my life anymore. But to see her with him of all people irked the piss right out of me. That and the fact that she had purposely avoided my eyes. There was no question; Merci was still in my blood; she was the sexiest women I'd ever known; even more so because she was so unaware of it and she was no longer my concern. I had to keep reminding myself of that fact.

I don't know how long I stood there staring at the empty spot where Masters' car had once been parked before I turned around and walked into the club. I climbed onto my usual stool at the bar and asked for my usual drink. God, I was predictable, and my life had been very dull until Merci had walked into it. Then why in Christ sake was I still sitting here? The answer was because of the child that Tricia and I were having.

Masters was up to no good. I wondered if he knew that Merci and I knew each other. Would she tell him, or maybe she already had? He was a bastard, and he loved rubbing my nose in something if it suited his purpose. He was still a good friend; I would find out soon enough how good his golf game was.

Merci

I avoided looking at Ryan as he and my boss continued to talk. If I hadn't had to use the ladies room just before we left, we wouldn't have run into him just outside the front door. It wasn't until Mr. Masters helped me into the back of the car before I felt comfortable enough to peek in Ryan's direction. He hadn't changed, he was still devastatingly gorgeous. He continued to watch as we drove out of the parking lot. Se la vie, he was no longer my concern, and the sooner I could convince myself of that the better off I would be. Try telling that to your heart.

Troy Masters chuckled to himself as we pulled out of the parking lot. "I enjoy rubbing things in Ryan's face. I enjoyed hearing your ideas, Merci. I believe Gregory Marx is infatuated with you. The old bugger wouldn't be a bad catch for a young, single woman such as yourself. But then you're not looking for looking for his type now, are you?"

"Excuse, me. Mr. Masters? I enjoy working, and I'm not looking for anyone who's either controlling or who wants to belittle me. I've had enough of living with someone who treated me like that to know better. I also don't appreciate anyone, even you Mr. Masters, making insinuations concerning my status. FYI, I just got out of one unhealthy relationship, and I have no intentions of jumping into another. I am quite happy with myself and with my life the way it is. Thank you very much."

"I apologize, Merci, I wasn't trying to insinuate anything. I'm glad to know you are happy with the way things are going. Now for your other ideas, what gave you the impression that Gregory Marx was looking for more than I had originally offered him? You were right, of course, but did he say something to you…?"

~~

"I'm not sure what you are asking me to do. I have two little girls; I can't leave them alone for that long."

"Merci, I pay you well, I can always demote you and ask one of the other girls who would jump at the chance to be my assistant. Many of them would be thrilled to make the trip with me. I'm sure most of them would love the chance to spend a few weeks on an island in the middle of the Caribbean. I will give you until tomorrow morning to decide."

It probably looked as if I was trying to catch flies. My chin hung almost on my chest watching my boss walk away from me. I knew he was right. I'd already heard many of the rumors that had gone around the office about me. They all figured I was sleeping with him. Who else moves that far up the ladder so quickly? Big jerk! Oh well. I was very grateful for the opportunity, and I was able to take care of my two children very well from the salary he was paying me. I still had my nest egg from Ryan, but I would only touch that if an emergency of some sort happened.

I finished up the project my boss had me working on before I left to take my lunch break. I had found a small little café that was close to the park. I loved going there to eat. It was a family owned place with great food and prices. Plus, they were friendly, and there was no chance I'd run into anyone I knew. I loved supporting small business as well.

I changed out of my high heels and into my flat shoes, so I could power walk. I absolutely loved my new freedom. I could do whatever I wanted and didn't have to answer to anyone, except Mr. Masters. But I did get paid for it. Still, I could buy clothes for the girls and me if we needed them, I could treat myself to lunch, and if I didn't feel like making food, I could bring home a kid's meal if I wanted to. I was happy despite the heartache and loneliness I felt occasionally. But the good in my life far outweighed the bad.

I tucked my high heels under my desk and hurried over to the elevators before Mr. Masters could see me leaving. He'd been very demanding lately, and I wanted to have lunch alone to think about his request, or rather his demands. I began my short walk. I'd become very adept at ignoring the catcalls and whistles as I hurried across the pavement. Men were all animals lusting after anything with a vagina. I decided it didn't matter what the person looked like; men saw a walking vagina and whistled hoping to see if it swallowed them up or something.

Ryan

I was on my second drink when my cell phone rang. "Masters, did you get everything from Cecelia? What's that supposed to mean?" The sly bastard was questioning me about, Merci. "I've seen her around. Actually, one of my gym buddies went out with her a few weeks ago. I happened to be at the club that night, that's all." I was bending the truth a little so that he wouldn't push the issue of Merci any further.

"Yes, she is a beautiful woman, but I know for a fact she has two little girls. Stay out of her life, Troy. She doesn't need your kind of trouble, nor mine." I didn't like where he was steering this conversation.

"Hey, before I forget, will you check on the island specs; I want to expand my operations there. I just need to know if there is anything that will prevent that from happening."

I listened to his questions with half my brain; the other half was listing the things I needed to take with me. "Sure, sounds good. I'll let you know when we get there. Sometime this weekend if everything goes according to my plans. Hey, I've got to go, Tricia is on the other line."

I looked at her name on the screen; then I put a smile on my face before I answered. "Tricia, are you all packed and ready to leave? Make sure you bring something sexy to wear to bed after I take you out dancing. Sebastián assured me there would be plenty to keep us entertained for a few weeks." I had to make this work between us for our child's sake, so I continued, "Tricia, I'm looking forward to spending time with you. I swear it will be better than it ever was before. I love you. See you soon."

I disconnected the call, then took a deep breath. "Oh, Merci, this trip better be the thing that is needed to erase you from my constant thoughts."

"Did you say something, Mr. West?"

"No, just muttering to myself. I think after I finish this drink, I'm all done for the afternoon and a for few weeks. Jake, could you do me a huge favor?"

"Sure, ask me anything."

"Do you remember that pretty blond that was in here a few weeks ago, the same one that was here by herself a few weeks before that?"

He nodded, "Who could forget that one? She was in here earlier with a group of businessmen."

"Yes, she's the one." I slipped a bill into his hand then asked, "If you see her in here with anyone or even by herself in the next few weeks could you make sure she doesn't drink too much?"

He smiled then pocketed the money. "No problem. I'll look out for her. I take it you won't be in here for a while?"

"Nope, I'm going to my island. I'm trying to work on expanding it. It's the perfect location, and with a little TLC, I think it will become one of my biggest moneymakers. The economy is looking up. People like a place where they can go and forget about their lives. Thanks, Jake. I'll see you when I get back."

Merci

I was very excited to get home to my girls. We were going shopping and then we were going to go to a movie. I wasn't kidding when I told my boss that I loved my life the way it was now. I could do whatever I wanted to do for myself and my sweet girls.

"Hey, I'm home, where are you both hiding?" My mother mouthed the words; *they want you to find them*, then she smiled. "Where could they be? Mom, did you see where they went?"

She played along. "I don't know, I turned around, and they were gone. You might look in the bedrooms."

I started down the hall calling out, "Who is going to go shopping with me now? I don't want to go by myself. I guess I could go to the movies and eat popcorn all alone."

I knew that would bring them running. "We're right here, mommy. Can we go to the movie with you? Please, we want popcorn, we want popcorn." They both started chanting together.

"There you are, I think I would like that very much, but our movie doesn't start until later. Can I interest you in doing a little shoe shopping with me?" They both smiled and nodded their heads. "Good. Maddie, will you help Allie change her pants. She needs something that fits her better. I need to ask grandma a question. Thank you, Maddie. Go with your sister, Allie."

My mom waited until the two girls had disappeared into their bedroom. "What is it, Merci, you look troubled?"

My mom knew me so well. "My boss has demanded that I go with him out of the country for a few weeks. It's all business of course, but I don't want to go."

"Then tell him no, Merci. Tell him you have two little girls who need their mama right now."

"I already did, and he threatened to demote me and take someone else. I make really good money now, Mom. I can't lose this job."

My mother smiled, "What do you want me to do, Merci? You know your father, and I adore those two girls. Do you want them to stay with us?"

"I'm only asking because I don't have anyone else to turn to. Could you, please!"

"Let me check with your father first, but I already know what he is going to say. Make sure you leave me all their pertinent information just in case of an emergency."

I saw my two girls walking down the hall toward me with huge smiles on their sweet faces. I reached over and hugged my mom. "Thank you so much. You and Papa, have done so much for us these last few months. Girls, give your grandma a big hug and kiss and tell her thank you for the fun day, then you can go play in your room, so grandma and I can talk before we go shopping."

Chapter Three

Ryan

"Tricia, are you feeling all right? We can re-schedule the trip if you aren't up for it." She looked pale as we sat in first class waiting for our turn on the runway. "It's not too late to turn back around."

She turned and smiled. "Thank Ry; you're the best. I can't wait to get back to the island. We haven't been there in a few years. Maybe you can take it easy on me for a few days while we're there. I think I'm in the worst stages of the pregnancy. Morning sickness really sucks."

I squeezed her hand. "I have no clue what you are going through, but I'll be as easy on you as I possibly can. Just let me know when you are ready for me again. I am more determined than ever to treat you like a queen." I picked up her hand and slowly kissed each of her knuckles.

"Thanks, Ry. I hope this crap goes away soon. I don't ever want to get pregnant again, by the way. So this baby better be what you want. I'm not giving you a do-over."

What was that supposed to mean? I dropped her hand and stared out the window. We were picking up speed, and would soon be in the air. It was too late to turn back now. I'd made my bed, and I was going to lie in it whether I wanted to or not.

"Hey, Ry, when we get to the island do you think we could have separate suites until I feel better?" I turned and stared at her. "Thanks, babe. I knew you would understand."

So much for her trying hard. "Sure, just let me know if you want me at all, would you? Hold on, here we go."

The next few hours were mostly spent in silence; Tricia and I didn't talk about our plans for the baby at all. I stared out the window while Tricia slept. The flight attendant came around for the fourth time and asked me if I wanted anything else to drink.

"Why not, bring me another one of these." I held up my mini bottle of bourbon.

"Would you like that with club soda?"

"No, give it to me straight up this time."

She had been trifling with me, and in my slightly inebriated and feeling sorry for myself state, I decided to flirt back. What did I have to lose? Tricia was sleeping, and I'd had no one at all to talk with. I glanced at her name badge, "Hey, Paulette, do you ever get a chance to stay on the island after one of your flights?"

"I have just once with my boyfriend." She glanced down at my sleeping wife before she finished speaking. "How long have you been married?"

I slowly nodded my head up and down. "Awe, I guess you could say long enough to know better. How much further do we have to go?"

"I believe we have another hour."

"Good, then I've got time for at least two more of these. Bring them both together and a tall glass of ice."

She nodded and hurried away from me. My mood had changed drastically, and I didn't care who knew it. She brought back the glass of ice and the two mini bottles. "Good luck, sir." Then she turned and hurried toward the other passengers who demanded her attention.

I poured both mini bottles into the ice and raised it above Tricia. "May we both come out of this alive!"

I finished my drink just before Paulette came around to gather any last-minute trash or other things before we were told to put our seat belts back on. I handed her my empty glass and the two bottles, then gave her a generous tip.

"She needs to be upright for the landing." She pointed at Tricia who was still asleep on the seat next to me.

"Thanks, you've been very helpful." I waved her away from me, then thought about how I would wake up my wife. "Tricia, come out come out wherever you are."

Tricia stretched out her arms above her head, then she opened her eyes and her nose wrinkled up at the same time. "Oh, my God, Ryan. You stink. What have you been drinking?"

"My dear wife, Bourbon whiskey, straight up, just in case you wanted to know."

"What an unpleasant way to wake up. Really, Ry. Don't you think about me at all? That smell is going to make me vomit."

"Can you wait until we get out of the plane at least, we're about to land."

Merci

"Mom, you are the best." I pulled her in close and hugged her tight. "You don't think dad will mind, do you?"

"Not at all, you know he adores these two little girls just as much as I do. I don't know if I mentioned it to you before, but Maddie is quite the fisherman. If we have a chance to take them camping while you are gone, we will do it. Just promise me that you will be safe, and don't do anything foolish."

"Of course not, I will avoid my boss while we are there at all costs when it comes to what you are thinking. I don't need any of that in my life yet. Besides, he isn't my type."

"You have a type now do you? My beautiful daughter, don't fall for any man who doesn't put you first. You don't need another Paul in your life either. Find someone like your father who will adore you and give you small little gifts to show you that you are loved daily. Someone who puts you first no matter what. Your father has spoiled me, and I want the same for you. I love you, little one."

"I love you too, Mom!" I put my arms around her, and we squeezed each other tightly. "I will be very careful, just think by this time in a few days I will be on my first tropical island. I will be working of course, but I will get some free time. I'm actually getting very excited about going. Especially knowing my girls will be well taken care of by the both of you. What would you like me to bring you and daddy back as a souvenir?"

"It might sound a little silly, but I've always wanted a real coconut from off a palm tree. If you can't find one of those where you are going, bring me chocolate."

"Thank you, Mom. I'm going to take my two little girls now and do some shopping. I don't have a swimsuit that fits me anymore, and I want them to have some new jammies for their *staycation* with their grandma and grandpa. I will see you in the morning. Have a good night, Mom."

"Maddie, please help Allie get her shoes back on her feet. I've almost got this suit on." I was trying on swimsuits; not one of them was appealing in any way shape or form. "Why is it that all one pieces look like they were made for old ladies. I'm not an old lady yet, am I?"

Maddie answered my rhetorical question. "No Mommy, you aren't old until you look like grandma. She's old, huh, Allie?"

"Maddie, that wasn't very nice. Grandma isn't that old, just older than me. How does this one look on me?" I had on a soft pink one-piece that shimmered.

"It makes you look not old like grandma, huh Allie?"

That made me giggle. "Well then, I guess we will move on to the next store. I can't find one here that I like at all. Allie, stand up and take your sister's hand." Allie was getting cranky. Shopping wasn't fun for the two of them at all, and she wouldn't be good during a movie either.

"Tell you what; you have both been such good girls, let's go to one of mommy's favorite places and get something to eat. Then if you both eat your dinner like good girls, we can have some dessert. I will go shopping tomorrow on my lunch break. How does that sound?"

"Yes, yes, yes. We like dessert, huh Allie?"

Allie put a big smile on her face. "Dessert, yes I wike dessert."

Ryan

Jameron Sebastián met us at the airport and loaded our luggage into the back of the limo. "Mr. and Mrs. West, it is so nice to have you stay with us. Mrs. West, you look as lovely as ever." He took her hands and leaned in to kiss both her cheeks, then he grasped my hand in his and shook it hard. "Boss man, do you want your usual suite of rooms on the beach?"

I glanced at Tricia. She was fanning herself with one of the pamphlets from inside the plane. "I would like that very much, Tricia, will you join me?" I already knew what her answer would be. She was pissed at me because I had been drinking on the plane, and she couldn't drink because of the pregnancy. At this point, I didn't care if we spent time together or not. I hadn't been here in a few years, and I planned to work, drink, and relax. I didn't care what order came first.

"I'd rather have my own space, if you don't mind, Ry. Then if I'm napping, I don't have to worry about you waking me up."

"You heard the lady, Sebastián. Do you want a cabana suite close to mine near the ocean, or would you prefer yours to be in the main hotel?"

"Really, Ry, do you have to even ask? I came here to get pampered, and the thoughts of waking back and forth in the sand to get my morning massage doesn't sound all that great. Jameron, can you find me one that is on one of the lower floors. Elevators aren't my thing right now. I'm expecting you know."

Sebastián looked back and forth between Tricia and me, then clapped me on the back. "Congratulations, Boss man, and you as well, Mrs. West. I knew you were glowing, and now I know why. When is the remarkable event going to happen?"

"I was wondering that myself, Tricia still hasn't told me when it will be. Tricia, you heard, Sebastián. When is the *remarkable* event going to take place? I want to celebrate the upcoming birth of my child with you while we are here on the island."

"I already told you once; doctor Humphries hasn't given me a specific date yet. He will know more when I go in for an ultrasound next month. We can still celebrate." Tricia walked up and put her arms around my neck and kissed me quickly on the mouth, then she pulled away, and I watched her nose wrinkle up before she spoke again. "Ryan, I do hope you drink something other than Bourbon while we are here. That stuff turns my stomach."

"Jam, if you are ready, let's get to the hotel, I've got a few things I need to look at before we make any other plans for this evening." He helped Tricia into the back seat of the limo, and I climbed in from the other side.

~~

Sebastián spoke a little on the way to the hotel while I studied the scenery as we drove along. The island had changed quite a bit since the last time we had been here.

I noticed there many more superstructures. A lot of glitz and promises of sun and fun posted on the billboards out front. I also knew that most of these larger hotels that were here didn't have the beachfront that we did. They offered a lot of amenities, but they didn't have the ocean to back them up. I had some great ideas, but I wished there was someone who was available here for me to use that could give me the feedback that I wanted, and that my property needed. I was more determined than ever to make sure I did the renovations on my property right.

We pulled into the circular driveway, and Sebastián helped us unload our baggage. My resort was a beautiful property, but compared to the ones that I had seen while we were driving, it was ready for that facelift. "Thank you, Sebastián. Tricia, let me get that bag for you."

Merci

After we had a small dinner, I took the girls to one of the exclusive shops where I had shopped before. The girls who worked inside immediately remembered me and after hearing what I was looking for went to work to find me the perfect suit.

My two girls were given snacks, and they had someone looking after them, so I could shop in comfort. I loved the perks that came with a little bit of money.

The same woman who had jumped through hoops to help me the last time I had been here approached me. "Mrs. Crandall, it's so nice to see you again. What can we help you with?"

"It's Bridget, correct?" She nodded, and I proceeded to tell her what it was that I was looking for and that I only had a day to find it.

"We must get your measurements first, Merci. Sophia will help you undress and then get them from you. Afterward, we can see what we have in the store that is ready made. You haven't given us much time to prepare."

"I know, I was informed of this opportunity today. I found nothing in a one piece at the last store we went into. I hope there is something that will work for me here."

"Why a one piece? You have a perfect figure and flawless skin." Bridget placed her finger on her chin and seemed to stare off into space. Then her face lit up, and she looked back at me with a sparkle in her eye. I knew at once I was in trouble.

"Sophia, when you are finished with Mrs. Crandall, meet me in the holiday shop please." She turned and sashayed into the other room, while Sophia pushed me into the large dressing room that I had been in the last time I had come. It was a bittersweet memory. But I had looked amazing in the short skirt and matching halter-top I had bought that night.

"Please disrobe, Mrs. Crandall."

"Do you think you could call me, Merci. It seems kind of weird to hear you call me that when I'm going to be standing here in my underwear in front of you."

"Of course, Merci. Your underwear must be removed as well. We need your precise measurements to make sure your swimwear fits you perfectly."

"Naked, you want me to stand here naked?" Sophia nodded without batting an eye. "Prepare, I have two girls you know, and I've got some bumps and bulges that shouldn't be there." I don't know what else I mumbled as she twirled me this way and that way and ran her tape measure across my goose bump covered skin.

"Merci, you have two girls, but one would never know. I for one would kill to have your boobs." She giggled at me after that. "Relax,

Merci. You've got nothing to worry about; you have a body that most women can only dream about. What is your secret?"

She continued her measurements and jotted down some numbers. I just stood there flabbergasted. She didn't mean that she probably told all the moms who came in here the same thing. I wasn't anywhere near dream worthy. Paul had mentioned that to me many times during our marriage. But now I did work out regularly, and I ate much healthier than I used to.

"I will be right back, Merci. You can slip on that robe and visit your two girls while we search for the perfect suit." She nodded at the fluffy white robe that hung on a hanger on the hook.

I put it on and tied the front before leaving the room to find my girls. I knew this place would be closing soon. I might have to settle for the first things they showed me so that I had something to take with me.

We only sat together for a few moments before, Bridget, told me she was ready for me. She smiled then said, "Mrs. Crandall, Sophia is ready for you in your dressing room. Your children are welcome to come and sit in the gallery and wait for your fashion show if they would like."

"Yes, yes, mommy. We want to see the fashion show." Maddie and Allie stood up from the floor and clapped their hands together.

"Fashion show? I just need a swimsuit."

Bridget smiled, "We found a few more things for you to try on. You must be prepared for the weather when you are going to a tropical island. I think your girls will enjoy the show. Go on inside, Merci."

I couldn't help but grin at the variety of things that were waiting for me to try on. I knew exactly what I had wanted to bring, and after seeing all that they offered to me, I decided to splurge. "Oh, my goodness, where do I begin? If I'm going to do this, ladies, then I'm going to do it right!"

Chapter Four

Ryan

I stayed with Tricia to make sure she was checked into her suite comfortably before I left with Jameron Sebastián to get myself settled into my own suite which was almost on the beach. Those beach suites were my money makers. I would do whatever it took to make sure I had more of the same to offer to my guests.

"Congrats, Ryan. You are going to be a father. I'm sure you are excited about the little one."

"Yes, I am. I just wish we had a date, so I could plan around it. We've got a lot to do here, and I wouldn't want to miss it. Jameron, we have many things to discuss. I must change out of my clothes and put something more comfortable on, so we can talk. I'll meet you at the beachfront bar."

"Yes, sir. I will see you there."

Jameron had been a good friend long before I offered him the job of general manager at this resort. I paid him well, but he earned it. He kept the Western Winds running smoothly for me. Maybe he knew of someone who could draw up the plans for more of the beach suites for me. I'd also asked if he knew a good contractor for the job.

Hurriedly I took off my pants and shirt and put on a nicer pair of jean shorts and a pullover shirt. I slipped into my sandals and slowly made my way to the bar. This property always got me excited. I wondered why It had taken me, so long to return.

I knew exactly where my property lines went. So before I met Jameron at the bar, I walked along the beach and made a mental note of how much space we would have to work with for the expansion. He was waiting for me at the bar with my usual drink in his hand.

"Thanks, Jam. This reminds me," I lifted my drink. "I want to offer more choices at all of the bars on my resort. Different names and different themes for each one. We've got a lot of work to do my friend. What are you drinking?"

"Rum and coke. I understand what you are suggesting, but what would you call this one?" Jam held up his glass.

I chuckled. "I don't know; we're boring and boring doesn't sell. Rum and coke with a splash of lime…how about a Citrus Bum? I can see the eyebrows raised now. But it would work. Now for the big guns, do you know anyone on the island that could help me re-design this place? We've got to keep up with the Joneses down the street. That mother fucker is huge."

Jameron shook his head slowly at me; I knew I was in for an earful. "I told you to come and visit ages ago, man. We still get repeat customers, but even on the beach, we can't offer the same as those Joneses are doing. I know no one who lives on the island who hasn't already been picked up by the competition. We need new blood in here, and someone who knows what the female tourists would like. They are the ones who make their man spend his money."

Jameron was a good-looking man. He was from the island of Jamaica originally but had lost some of his accent when he moved to America. I knew he could turn it on when he wanted to impress the ladies. "Jameron, do you currently have a lady friend? Maybe she could be our Guiney pig until we find someone else. We do need a woman's point of view."

"What about Mrs. West, is she not qualified for that position? You are selling her short, Ryan."

How did I say what I needed to say without him getting the wrong idea? "Jameron, we've known each other for a long time. Listen, I love, Tricia, but I don't want her involved in this precise project. This is my baby. Western winds was always a dream of mine as a young man. Don't get me wrong, I'm sure Tricia has some great ideas, but I just don't want them implemented in my resort."

"I get you, man. Not to worry, I don't say a word. I'll have another Citrus Bum bartender."

"I like that, it sounds beachy, right?" We spent the next few hours talking about the resort and other things that were happening on the island. I needed to get a report typed up and sent to Troy before he left to come here. He was supposed to arrive either late Saturday evening or early Sunday morning.

"Make sure you put Troy in a room of his choosing; he hates the beach by the way. I'd better check on Tricia and see what she wants to eat for dinner. Hopefully, her morning sickness has gone away. I'll see you later, Jam."

Merci

I was packed and ready to go. I understood why Troy masters wanted me to go with him. He informed me that he liked my fresh ideas and that I would be a great resource to have on our trip to the Caribbean islands. He was sending his car for me, and it should be here very soon.

"Come here you two!" I waited for my two mopey girls to give me a hug and a kiss. Maddie was pouting, and Allie was imitating her for my benefit. "If you don't give me a kiss and hug now then we will all be sad. I won't be gone very long, but I will miss each one of your kisses so much. Please!"

Allie rushed into my arms, and Maddie followed her. Mommy, why can't we go too?" I recognized her tone of voice; she was tired. That is why she was so whiney.

"Maddie, I will take you next time. This time I will be working. When we go on a vacation together, I want to have you both just for me. I don't want to share with anyone. Please be good for grandma and grandpa." I kissed them hard on their cheeks, then I stood up and hugged and kissed both my parents.

"I'm not sure whether or not my phone will work from the Caribbean. I will give you a call when we get there with a number that you can reach me at if you need me. I'll try to call you when I can so I can talk to my girls." Just then we all heard the knocking at the front door.

I quickly kissed them all one more time, then grabbed my two bags and walked over to the front door. I opened it to find Troy Masters waiting for me. "Oh, I didn't expect to see you here. Would you like to meet my family?"

He made a strange face, then stepped just inside the door. He stuck his hand out and reached for my fathers to shake it. "It's nice to meet you both. Merci, are these your two girls? They are just adorable. We need to hurry, Merci. I will take good care of her, folks."

Troy bent over and picked up both of my bags, then turned and walked back out the way he came in. "Goodbye, I will call you when I get there. Thank you!" Troy loaded my bags into the trunk, before helping me into the back seat of his limo. I continued waving at my girls until they were out of my site.

I hadn't realized I was crying until my boss said something to me. "You won't be gone for too long, Merci. They look like they are in good hands. Cheer up; I need your happy face on for this trip. Are you sure that you've packed enough for two weeks?"

I wiped my nose on a tissue that I found in my purse. "Always prepared, that's me. Yes, I have enough for two weeks. I don't need much."

"Surprising, that's all. Most woman I know would have more than just two small bags. I hope you brought more to wear than your bikinis. We will have a few business meetings while we are there. I'll give you the folder to read once we are in the air. I'm counting on you, Merci. Do me a favor, once we get there, could you please refer to me as Troy? It's more of a relaxed atmosphere, and it wouldn't hurt my reputation by having a beautiful girl such as yourself on my arm."

I started to say something, but we had arrived at the airport. Troy helped me from the car, and his driver put both our bags on the curb before he called for a porter. "Mr. Masters, I will call you Troy when we are around your friends, but I still think I should address you properly when we are in a business setting."

"It won't be a business setting; we will be in the Caribbean. Merci, I insist; it's an order. Come, let's get checked in."

I felt comfortable with Troy Maters, and if he insisted, then I guess I would have to obey him. He was my boss. Still..."How long is the flight, Troy?"

He smiled when he heard me say his name. "That wasn't so hard now, was it, Merci? We've got a five-hour flight ahead of us, so sit back and relax once we are situated on the plane. We will get there late tonight, but we will be able to work on things early in the morning. We are flying first class, so if you would like something to drink or perhaps something to snack on, let me know."

"Thank you, Troy. I might be ready for a snack later, but I can use the time to catch up on my sleep. After I look at those papers first of course."

Ryan

It was late when I sent Jameron to the airport to pick up Troy. We had gone over the entire resort today. I had made quite a few notes, and Jameron had given me many great suggestions as well. Still, I agreed that having a woman in the mix would be beneficial. I wanted to wait up for Troy, but I was tired. Maybe Tricia would consider having dinner with me tonight. It wouldn't hurt to ask.

I went into the main building and bypassed the elevators to climb up to the first floor where her suite was located. I stood outside and knocked. "Tricia, would you like to join me in the dining room for dinner? It's island food night." I almost started to knock again, when the door flew open.

"Island food? That sounds disgusting, Ry. Is that all they have?"

I didn't think she was eating enough, and I had wondered whether or not that type of food would sound appealing to her. "We can go outside to the beach café. How do burger and fries sound? Tricia, I'm worried that you aren't getting enough to eat. You've got to take better care of yourself. They offer soup in the café, and it's better than nothing at all."

I stepped into her room. She was still dressed, but her hair was a little unkempt. "I'll wait for you, and we can go down there together."

She breathed in through her nose then wiggled her pursed lips around at me before she answered. "Okay, I guess the fresh air would help too. I'll go and change my top; then I'll be right out."

She disappeared into the bathroom and shut the door. I was interested in this pregnancy; I didn't want her to shut me out. "Tricia, I would like to watch your body change, you know throughout the whole thing. Would you open the door? I have seen you naked recently you know. Let's make this special. I want to be a part of everything, and that includes going with you to your doctor appointments. Please, Tricia, open the door."

She did, but she had already changed her shirt and was in the process of brushing through her hair. "Ry, I'm not ready for you to see me yet. I hate getting fat. Maybe later in the pregnancy when it looks like I'm expecting and not fat. I hate having a pooch. For now, can we just agree not to bring it up? I'm starving; you mentioned soup."

I turned away from her. I was disappointed, but I didn't want it to affect the mood of the night. I smiled before I looked back at her. "Promise me that I will be able to escort you to your next doctor visit. Promise me, Tricia or I will get all petulant and grumpy." I took her hand and pulled her in close to nuzzle the side of her neck. "You don't want me grumpy, do you?"

"Stop, I'm starving. You don't want me to be grumpy either." She linked her arm with mine and pulled me out into the hallway. "I need food, and you are going to get it for me. Do they still have a band on Saturday nights? I remember when we first came here, and it played all night long just for us. Do you remember?"

I allowed her to lead the way. "That seems like a lifetime ago, Tricia. If there is one playing tonight, will you dance with me? I don't remember the last time we danced together."

"We will see. Hurry, Ry. Maybe we can go swimming in the pool tomorrow. I bought a new maternity swimsuit to try out."

"You don't need one of those yet. You aren't that far along yet, Tricia."

"I told you I was getting fat. I think some woman get a pooch must faster than others do. If you are embarrassed, we don't have to go." She was sullen now; I hated that more than anything else she did.

"I didn't say that, Tricia. We will go swimming, but I don't think you need a maternity swimsuit already. That is all I was saying. You still look wonderful. I can't wait to see you as you get further along."

We continued to chat together amicably until we reached the beach café. The new tentative name of the café that Jam and I had come up with was *'The Beach spray.'* We needed to change the menu and offer different food items to keep the interest of the guests. The beach-themed drinks would also be provided in here as well as the new bar. We would continue to provide live music most of the nights, and Jam knew of someone who might be interested in becoming our new event specialist. They would work on entertainment for the guests as well as the variety of entertainment we showcased in the restaurant and the beach café once it was remodeled and had changed over to the new name and theme.

I asked for a table outside on the beach for us to sit and have our dinner. "Is this okay, Tricia? The fresh air will do us both good tonight. I'm famished. Jameron and I went over the entire property today. There needs to be changes made, and it will involve a lot of cash, but with all the other resorts nearby it will be a worthwhile investment. What kind of food are you in the mood for?"

Chapter Five

Merci

I didn't know how long I had been asleep, but I woke up with the airplane making its descent onto the island. I opened my window and watched the scenery flashing below us. It was late at night, but I saw so many properties around the island that were lit up.

A voice over my shoulder asked, "What do you think, Merci? It's entirely something else to see at night, isn't it?"

"It is beautiful. The water looks unreal with the moon shining on it. Wow, I can't believe I am here."

I continued to watch uninterrupted until the flight attendant announced over the speakers that it was time to make sure our seats were in an upright position while they finished cleaning up any trash that we might still have. Then she thanked us and told us the time in Saint Lucia was one a.m. and the current temperature was seventy-five degrees with a light breeze from the south.

I sat up straight in my seat and prepared for our arrival. This was a smaller plane than I had been on before. It only had fifty passengers. I wondered how landing would be in it. Not that I was an expert on flying, but I had traveled to France with my parents once when I was younger.

The planed landed very smoothly, and I glanced around to make sure I had everything before we were ready to depart.

Troy stood up and let me pass in front of him; then I felt his firm hand on my lower back as we left the plane and walked down the outside steps onto the tarmac. The pavement was lit up, but I stumbled a little.

"I've got you, Merci. Do you need a moment to adjust?" He chuckled then continued, "It's an odd feeling when you first step off a plane onto an island. It almost feels as if you are floating and you may need to find your sea legs. There should be someone waiting to pick us up in front of the airport. If you need to sit down once we are inside, we can take a few minutes for you to do so."

"I've got this; I think you are right. It did seem to feel as if we were swaying a bit. I can't wait to get to the hotel; I am exhausted. Have you stayed there before?" We continued to make small talk as we went to get our luggage from the airport concierge. It only took a few minutes for them to load it onto a cart and push it outside where a limo with the name 'Western Wind' was written inside a picture of a lush tropical setting, and partially covered the side of the Limo.

A tall, dark, gorgeous man stood leaning against the car with his ankles crossed, and his hand resting on the top of the vehicle. He had on khaki shorts and a matching pullover shirt; he wore sandals on his feet.

I didn't expect the velvet sound of his voice as it tickled my senses. "Mr. Troy Masters, it has been a long time, sir. Who is this vision by your side?"

Troy chuckled, then shook the man's hand before he took my wrist and pulled me forward. "Jameron Sebastián, this beautiful young lady is my assistant, Merci Crandall. I hope you can find accommodations for her at the hotel. It was a last-minute decision to bring Merci with me."

Well, that was awkward. I hadn't realized that I had been a last-minute decision. That wasn't what Troy had made it sound like at all. "Mr. Sebastián, it is so nice to meet you." I stuck my hand straight out in front of me as I spoke.

He took my hand in his as I was rewarded with his throaty musical sounding laugh. "You must call me, Jameron. Is it Miss, or Mrs. Crandall?" His brown eyes twinkled at me which made me smile and put the awkwardness between us to rest immediately.

"Jameron, you can call me Merci, I insist."

"Mlle, faites vous parlez le français?" His French was impeccable.

"Oui Je fais. You speak French very well, Jameron."

"Le Merci manque, ma mère était le français et c'était elle qui m'a enseigné. And you, miss?"

Troy interrupted our conversation. "This meeting of yours, can we finish it once we start driving. I remember you saying you were exhausted, Merci."

"I am sorry, Mr. Masters. I don't have the pleasure of meeting such a beautiful woman very often. Let me put your bags in the trunk, and we will be on our way." He did as he said he would before helping me into the back seat while Troy got into the car from the other side and sat beside me.

"How far is the drive from here, Jameron?" I sat back in the comfortable seats and looked around me as he drove.

"In the daytime, it takes forty-five minutes, but this time of night it will be much quicker. Thirty-five at the most. Merci, would you prefer a room inside the main building or would you like a suite on the beach?" He glanced at me from the rear-view mirror as he spoke.

"The beach? Right by the ocean? Oh my goodness, are you kidding me. The beach, do you even have to ask?" I hadn't even considered where we would be staying beforehand. This would be a dream vacation in every sense of the word; correction, a working dream vacation.

 Troy answered me. "I can't sleep with the sound of the waves crashing on the rocks that are near the beach. I prefer a suite in the top of the hotel where they are barely audible. The views of the island are spectacular from on top. Choose wisely, Merci."

"Jameron, which one would you recommend?"

"That is easy, Merci. Which calls to you most, the views or the ocean?"

"The ocean."

Ryan

I tried to stay up so that I could accompany Jameron to the airport, but he insisted on driving alone. "Ryan, you look tired my friend. Get some sleep; your pretty wife seems to have worn you out at dinner. I will pick up your friend and make sure he is taken care of. Tomorrow is another day, and we can meet at the restaurant for breakfast before we go over more of the property."

"Jam, you are a lifesaver. You never answered me when I asked earlier. Do you have a lady friend on the island?"

"I had someone six years ago, but she didn't want to be here anymore. She said it was too isolated for her and went back to America. I did not."

"I'm sorry old friend, if you weren't married to my resort would you have followed her?"

"I thought about that many nights. The answer is no. I miss the islands, and the ocean calls to me. I could only be here. If she loved me enough to stay, I might have compromised in the future, but she didn't want compromise. Good night, Ryan West. I will see you in the morning."

I thought about what Jameron had said after he left. Compromise was essential in any relationship. Did I do enough of that with Tricia? We had to make this marriage work for the baby's sake.

As soon as Jameron left, I made myself a drink and sat down outside on my private patio with it to think. I don't know how long I stared at the water, but I had finished my drink. I set my empty glass on the table, then went inside to take a shower.

I slept better here than I ever did back home. Even when I stayed up late, the sleep I got was rejuvenating. A hot shower would wash away the aches that I had in my muscles, but it wouldn't erase the need I had.

I stripped out of my shorts and climbed into the large outside shower. I was isolated out here, but it was more than isolation that I felt. I was lonely. I wanted someone in here with me. I turned the water up a notch, then took care of my basic needs. Merci's face filled the fog in my brain, and I could have sworn I heard her laughter as I continued to milk my member.

I climbed out of the shower and dried off inside, then I slid into my cool sheets and fell asleep with Merci's face still in my mind, and the memory of her lush body tormenting my dreams.

~~

The sun played peek-a-boo as it teased me through the slats in the window shades. I didn't know what time it was except for daylight. I decided to forgo another shower and instead went into my well-equipped kitchen and started myself a cup of coffee on the Keurig. The digital time over the stove read seven-seventeen as I grabbed my cup and went outside to sit in the comfortable chair on my beach-facing patio.

It was a beautiful Sunday morning, peaceful, calm, and clear azure blue skies. I loved waking up like this. I remembered what Jameron had said about his lady friend and wondered if Tricia would be okay with moving here permanently. I doubted it, but I could always ask. It would give us both a new beginning, and there would never be a chance of running into my past mistakes.

But she wasn't a mistake. Merci had been there when I needed her most, and I would hope that I had been the same for her. From the looks of her just the other day she looked happy and prosperous, and still hotter than any woman I had ever known. I had to move on; there would be no more crying over spilled whiskey.

I glanced down the beach and saw Jameron walking towards me, in his arms he carried a bundle. I almost stood up to wave him over to where I sat when he disappeared around the corner of the next suite over from mine. We had arranged to meet for breakfast; he probably had a few things to take care of before then. He was the general manager, and he still had work to do while I could play.

I heard his laughter ring out from next store; then I heard a woman's laughter. That wasn't any woman. Merci? That wasn't possible; she was back in the United States running things for Troy while he was here on business with me. Then I heard it again.

"Merci!"

Merci

It was paradise. Absolute, freaking crazy paradise. Jameron showed me to my suite after checking both Troy and me into the hotel. He set my luggage by the front door before he showed me where everything was located, then stayed to teach me how to turn on the Television and the stereo as if I would waste any of my time sitting in front of the TV.

He carried my luggage into the bedroom then opened the door into the bathroom. "Come, Merci. There is something you should see."

I enjoyed listening to the man talk; he still had a slight Jamaican accent that was to die for. He was gorgeous on top of that, so hearing him say come had me eagerly rushing over to what he was trying to show me.

"What is it, Jameron?"

"It is something that only the beach suites have. It's an outdoor shower, but not to worry, if you feel uncomfortable the other bedroom in the suite has one that is private and located inside." He smiled and waved me past him.

I walked outside and stood in the rocky outdoor shower and giggled. "Now this is something you don't see every day."

I hurried back inside; it felt a bit sinful to be standing there with his hotness just inches away. "Thank you, Jameron. I will keep that in mind. I followed him back to the front door and asked, "I'm not sure if I tip you or not. I don't have any change, but I can get some tomorrow."

"That would be an insult, Merci. Make sure you wake up in the morning and sit outside to have your coffee on your patio. The views of the sunrise coming up over the ocean are breathtaking."

It was then that I realized I had forgotten something. "I forgot to bring a robe, does the hotel have one that I can borrow? I don't want to flash the neighbors, or to scare them first thing in the morning."

"Miss Crandall, you are a lovely woman, and I will bring you a robe in the morning, so we don't have all the neighbors beating at your door and begging to come in. Is seven too early?"

"Not at all, it will give me a chance to get myself together before the rest of Mr. Masters group gets here." I thought I'd see how much French Jameron understood. "Le petit déjeuner dans le lit semble délicieux."

"If that is what you wish, Merci I can arrange for breakfast to be served to you in bed."

I knew I had turned beet red. "That had sounded quite provocative. Um, sorry, I think I said that wrong."

Jameron smiled at me, then walked out the front door. He turned and said, "I will bring your robe at precisely seven-fifteen. If you are still asleep, I will leave it at your door. Goodnight, Miss Crandall."

I watched until he was out of my sight. "Phew, I always loved me some hot chocolate. Get to bed, Merci; seven fifteen will be here way too soon." But I did have something sweet to look forward to. I quickly shed my clothes, then crawled under the silky sheets. I'd loved sleeping in sheets just like these when I'd spent the night with Ryan at a hotel a few months past. "Hmm, I guess money can buy a good night's rest. Go to sleep, Merci."

Chapter Six

Merci

The sun pushing its way in between my eyelids interrupted the dream I had been having. I stretched my arms up over my head and lay in bed for just a few minutes. I didn't get the morning sun in my bedroom back home.

"Oh, crap!" I looked around the room for a clock and couldn't see one, so I jumped up and ran into the living room to look for the time. Jameron said he would be here at seven-fifteen with a robe. The clock on the sleek white mantle above the cozy fireplace read **'7:13'** He would be here any minute and I was running around in my nothing. I rushed back into the bedroom and searched for something I could put on before he arrived.

There was a light rapping on the door, and I heard Jameron's rich voice call my name from the other side of the front door. I sped over to the bed, and pulled the lightweight cover off the top and wrapped it around me, then hurried into the living room with a white train dragging behind me.

I opened the door and almost fell on top of the man who was bent over in front of me. It took a few seconds for us both to figure out which way was up, and when I saw the look on his face, I laughed out loud. "I'm so sorry, Jameron. That could have been ugly if I had gone any faster."

His knowing brown eyes skimmed quickly over me, then he replied with just a bit of humor in his tone, "Miss Crandall, if you had landed anywhere behind me wrapped in that, I can assure you there would have been a riot of men fighting to save you. Here is your robe and I believe it is just in time."

I giggled again. "You, Jameron are good for my self-esteem. Would you please call me, Merci? I'm working on changing the Crandall part back to my maiden name."

"And what would that be, Merci?"

"Lachance. My father is French, and my mother is Spanish. I got my fair looks from her, and my name from my father. Both the first name and the last." We still stood outside on the small cement slab talking. I had forgotten that I wore next to nothing under my blanket, and stepped back into my suite.

"Miss Lachance, I will let you get dressed, I am sorry to have disturbed you. Breakfast will be at the main hotel this morning at nine a.m. It will be at Sea Breeze restaurant. Mr. Masters wanted me to let you know he is expecting you at that time."

"Thank you, Jameron." Suddenly I felt shy. "I will find it I'm sure. Thanks again for bringing me this robe. I'd best change into it before I get complaints from the rest of the vacationers wandering the beach."

"No complaints, Merci. Only jealous women who would keep their men from gazing at your lovely features. I will see you at breakfast." After saying that, Jameron turned and continued his walk on the beach.

"Oh, Lordy! That man is hot." I could look all I wanted; I was a single woman with two adorable girls and, I could look all I wanted. I hadn't realized I was grinning until I glanced up to see my reflection in the oversized bedroom mirror. I dropped the bedcover and studied my reflection more thoroughly. I was only twenty-six, but I had toned my body a lot in the last few months. I weighed less than I had when I first married Paul. I was still self-conscious of the stretch marks on my breasts and tummy, but they were dedicated to my sweet girls, and I wouldn't give them up for anything. I wasn't perfect, but I did feel a little better about the way I looked now.

The ladies at the store had all been very flattering when I tried on the different bikinis and other summer attire they had in my size. They were knowledgeable at what they did, and the items they had chosen for me to try on would have never been things I would have picked on my own. But each little scrap of a bikini I brought with me and the other things I splurged on looked okay on me. Besides, who would ever see me here in them except for my boss, and I didn't plan on doing any swimming or sunbathing when he was anywhere near.

I picked up the fluffy robe and put it on, then went into my kitchen to get me a cup of coffee. Once it was ready, I picked up my cup and stepped out onto my patio and sat down. Paradise. The beach was mostly empty, and the ocean waves rolling onto the shore were calming and mesmerizing. I don't know how long I had sat there before I felt like someone was watching me.

Ryan

I couldn't believe my eyes; it was her. "Merci, what are you doing here?" She looked so beautiful sitting on her patio with the morning sun radiating off her skin.

She started choking on the mouthful of coffee. "Ryan? Ryan? What are you doing here?"

"Me? What are you doing here? Wait, did Masters bring you with him?" She slowly nodded her head. "That son of a bitch. What in the hell was he up to?"

Merci stopped choking then in a disbelieving voice said, "You asked Troy to come here?"

Things must have progressed between the two of them if they were on a first name basis which really pissed me off. I had known Troy for as long as I could remember, and he was a stickler at work for formalities. "Yes, I did." Merci apparently still didn't know who I was.

We both grew quiet; I didn't want to say more than I had to, and she must have been embarrassed for me to know who she was here with. "Listen, Merci, this will be difficult for us both, but I hope you can enjoy your time here. I'm meeting Troy for breakfast at the hotel. My wife will be with me as well. I...I don't want things to be uncomfortable between us. I just thought you should know that my wife and I are expecting our first child."

She was quick to answer. "I had heard that from Zane. I'm not here to cause you problems, Ryan. I won't mention anything about that night, and I haven't. I didn't thank you properly for your gift. Thank you. Should I see if they can move me to another spot?"

I wanted to yell out yes and no. If she were to move into the hotel, she'd be more likely to run into Tricia. I wondered if Tricia would recognize her as the hooker who came to our hotel room. She wasn't a hooker, but Tricia didn't know that. I ran my hand back and forth over the top of my head. This was possibly the worst scenario that could have happened here on the island.

"No, I like having you nearby. We are friends, right? At least I hope we can be. It's up to you, Merci. I know Troy prefers being in the hotel; he hates the sand." I moved a bit closer to her, then leaned in closer to speak. "I swear I will leave you alone, and I never meant to hurt you the last time we saw each other. I want only the best for you, but you need to understand that I will do anything that I have to make sure my child and my wife don't get hurt."

"Ryan, it was never my intention to hurt anyone. Can you pretend that we are just acquaintances? I can if you can. But what if your wife recognizes me if we happen to run into each other while I'm here? That could be very awkward for all of us."

"Just tell her you are with Troy, I'm sure she didn't pay enough attention to you for her to even remember seeing you. Not that you are forgettable." That was the wrong thing to say; the vision of her lying nude on top of her bed in those ridiculous blue high heels popped into my head. I had to swallow hard before I could speak again. "Take care, Merci. I hope we will see each other around, enjoy your stay."

I waved at her, then hurried past her suite to find my way to the hotel and fetch my wife for breakfast. I could only hope that Troy would leave Merci behind when we met for breakfast to discuss business.

Merci

I jumped up and ran inside. I couldn't sit there and watch him walk away. *Forgettable?* That made me angrier than if he'd spit in my face. Ryan was lucky that I wasn't a vindictive person. I could sure ruin his life if I had been. But I wouldn't do that to another woman nor to a child. He wanted to be a father; I could see it in his eyes and I'd clearly heard it in the tone of his voice when he spoke. Ryan would make a good father.

I hadn't told him I would be there for breakfast. It was supposed to be a breakfast meeting for business. I assumed Ryan was able to do business while he was on vacation with his wife. He would be able to write it off that way. Oh well, I would avoid him every chance that I had, but I was here on business with my boss, and there was nothing Ryan could do to stop that from happening.

After putting away my things in the drawers, I hung my business outfit and dresses in the enormous walk-in closet. I chose a pretty violet sundress and matching sandals to wear to breakfast, then gathered my things and went into the bathroom to get ready. I'd forgotten all about the outdoor showers.

I could study the shower now in the light of day. It was almost the size of a small bedroom. The walls were of natural polished stone, and there was a small ledge on one side. The enclosure was at least eight feet high with two rainshower shower heads across from each other.

I set my hair products on the ledge then turned on the water, so it could heat up. I shed my robe and placed it on the chair then walked outside into the water. It felt sinful to stand under the hot spray, outside, and completely naked. I took my time washing and rinsing my hair; this was a new experience for me. One of many firsts that I knew would happen in the next few weeks. As I stood there I imagined how sensual it would be to shower with a man outside like this; one, in particular, came to mind.

I took a few more minutes to let the conditioner soak into my hair, then started to rinse it off when I heard Ryan's voice. He and Jameron were having a conversation. I quickly shut off the water; I didn't know if they could hear the sound of the shower water running, but as wicked as this felt already, having two men standing nearby listening made it even more so. I stood still and couldn't help but overhear their conversation.

"Long story my friend. She is a lovely young woman, but I can't have her upsetting Tricia."

Were they talking about me?

"I understand, sir. Would you like me to handle it? I can force her to leave. I've handled woman such as her before."

What? I glanced down, going from the hot steamy water and now standing outside wet in the early morning had left me covered in goosebumps, and I had two torpedoes for nipples at this point. I hoped the two men would leave soon so I could finish rinsing off my hair and resume my shower. I caught the tail end of something slithering on the ground by my feet. I screamed and screamed as I hopped from side to side in the rock shower.

Ryan

Jameron and I were discussing one of the new employees who had been arguing with Tricia earlier this morning. Tricia was fit to be tied when I met her in her room. The young woman had been arguing with Tricia over having extra towels put in her suite. I knew Tricia's habits, and she bathed twice a day. She wanted fresh towels every time she showered. The young woman was trying to tell her that it was wasteful, and she didn't have time to run back and forth to do her bidding.

I didn't want that kind of an employee working for me at this resort; she chose the wrong person to argue with. I had another question to ask Jameron when I heard a woman screaming; it sounded like Merci.

"Did you hear that?" She continued to scream. "Merci!" I ran toward the front door of her suite with Jameron following close behind me.

I started pounding on her door, "Merci, open the door."

Jameron pulled a bulky set of keys from his pocket. "I've got the master keys here, let me find the right one."

"Hurry, Jam, that doesn't sound good." He opened the door, and we both ran into her suite. We heard her screams once again coming from the master bedroom, and we both rushed into that room.

"Merci, where are you?"

Her terrified answer came from the bathroom. "I'm in the shower. Ryan, please hurry!"

Jameron and I both ran into the bathroom without knowing what was wrong. My heart dropped somewhere by my ankles when I saw Merci standing completely nude in the outdoor shower. There was an enormous boa constrictor blocking the doorway out. Merci was sobbing as she stood there naked, soaking wet, and shaking.

Jameron's calm voice resonated behind me, "Miss Lachance, do not move. I want you to reach behind you and slowly turn the cold water on; just a trickle for now. Turn it on. Good girl. When I come back with something to put over the snake, I will have you turn the tap on all the way. Full blast, the St. Lucia Boa likes to be warm, and this one entered the shower to regulate his body temperature. The cold water will cause him to recoil, but I must find something that I can throw over him so Ryan can get you out. Do not change the temperature or he will make his way toward you. You must remain calm, Merci. We will get you away from him safely. Ryan will you please keep talking to her."

He caught my eye; I understood how vital it was to keep her calm. "Merci, it will just be a few more minutes. You know which knob you must turn when Jameron is ready, right?"

She glanced at the knobs behind her, then turned her head back toward me and nodded rapidly. "Okay sweetheart, Jameron should be right back." I was worried about her going into shock; a boa constrictor wasn't something you saw every day. She was shivering, under the chilly water and I could see the gooseflesh covering her body.

I took a deep breathe then continued to talk to her. "Merci, look at me."

"I...I ca...can't."

I wanted to rush into the shower, pick her up and hold her tight to stop her from shaking. "Merci, it will be okay, here comes Jameron now."

Jameron stepped up behind me carrying a large blanket. "Merci listen to me, girl. When I tell you to turn on the cold water, do it then quickly move in opposite direction from the snake. Ryan, as soon as I drop this on the boa, get in there and get the girl out of there as fast as you can. Take her into the spare bedroom and wrap her in the sheets to get her warmed up. I have called Slaps, and they will be here soon to pick up the snake. You stay with that girl and make sure she doesn't go into shock."

"That's exactly what I had been worried about. Whenever you are ready, Jam."

Jameron calmly said, "Turn on the water now, Merci."

Chapter Seven

Merci

I don't know how I remained calm enough to focus, but having Ryan standing close to me had been the only thing keeping me from completely losing it and becoming hysterical. I heard Jameron say now, and I turned on the faucet on all the way. Immediately I felt two strong arms pick me up and I was carried through the rest of the rooms and into the spare bedroom. He laid me gently on the bed; I was still in a daze. I watched him remove his clothes, then he climbed onto the bed next to me and pulled the covers over the two of us. He pressed his warm body against me and started making soothing noises in my ear.

I don't know how long we lay together like that or when I finally stopped shaking. He tried to pull away from me, and I clung to him.

"Merci, I promise I will return. I need to meet Slaps with Jameron, I've got some questions that I must ask them. You seem to have warmed up, and you're not shaking as much." He kissed me on the brow then got out of the bed and quickly dressed. He gave me a quick smile before he walked out of the room and closed the door.

I was still cold, that had been the most terrifying thing that had ever happened to me. My two girls could have been motherless in an instant. It probably would have been a slow horrible death. I thought back to what happened; I don't know how I had missed seeing the giant snake in the shower. Maybe it had been in the bedroom or on the other side of the rock wall. I just knew I couldn't stay out here on the beach after that experience.

That hadn't been the only thing that had happened; I stood there under freezing water in my birthday suit with two grown men staring at every inch of me through the whole thing. I was mortified, how did I face either one of them after that? I wrapped the bed sheets tighter around me.

I heard the knocking on the front door; then I listened to the muffled voices of the men speaking. I couldn't hear what they were saying, but I knew I wasn't moving from this spot except to pack my things and move to the main hotel. Now I understood why my boss had wanted a room near the top floor. I'll bet they don't find snakes up there.

Eventually, I started to doze off but was startled back awake by the voices right on the other side of my door. Finally, it grew quiet again; too quiet. Had Ryan left me here alone?

There was a light knock at the door, then Ryan opened it and poked his head inside. "How are you doing, Merci? I've still got to meet Troy for breakfast. Do you need anything before I go?"

Panic hit me hard. "You are leaving me here? You can't go, Ryan. I can't stay here, not after finding th…that snake. Please don't leave me."

He hurried back over to the bed and climbed on top of the covers, and lay down next to me. His eyes followed his finger as he gently placed it on my chin. "Merci, the snake, has been removed, that won't happen again. It has never happened before, and I'm so sorry that it happened to you." He focused on my eyes. "When I saw you standing there knowing the snake could turn on you at any moment my heart stopped."

Ryan cupped my cheek in his hand. "Merci, I couldn't bear the thought of ending things between us without telling you how much I enjoyed our time together. I'm going to be a father; I hope you can understand why I let you go the way I did."

I didn't realize that I was crying until he ran his thumb under my eye and caught one of the tears with it. "Please don't cry, Merci."

"I'm not, at least not for the reason you think I'm crying for. I need to use the bathroom, and I'm afraid of what I might find in there." That was true, I did need to pee, but I would never let him know how much he hurt me again. "Would you please check the bathroom to make sure I'm safe? Also check carefully inside the shower, I still need to rinse my hair off."

Ryan

Poor Merci. This had been a shock for her. I didn't know how she would be able to sleep at night without seeing that snake in her dreams. But what could I do about it?

"I will make sure there is nothing inside, and I can assure you that you finding the snake in the shower was something that has never happened before and won't happen again. I'm sorry, Merci." I wanted to kiss her full pouty mouth hard and long and knew if I didn't get off the bed soon that is exactly what would happen.

I jumped up and hurried into the bathroom and look around like she had asked me to do. "There is nothing here, do you want to come and see for yourself?"

"I believe you. My clothes and shower things are still in the other bathroom, can you get them for me? I can't; I just can't go back in there right now."

"Sure, I will be right back. You can get in the shower and I can either leave them out here on the bed or set them inside the bathroom on the vanity. I'll be right back, Merci."

I made my way back to the master suite and saw her clothes in the bathroom where she had left them. I gathered her things from the shower first and took them to the other room where she was still lying in bed.

My throat felt dry; I needed a drink. "I'll set these inside there for you."

"Thanks, Ryan. Can you get my clothes too?"

"Yes, I'm on my way."

I left her laying there and took my time getting her clothes. I picked them up and held them to my face breathing deeply. I remembered that she wore the perfume called *Beautiful*. I dropped something lacy on the floor and bent over to pick up the purple bit of nothing. Our first night spent together in my hotel came to mind, and remembering Merci wearing the underwear from Victoria's, almost the same color as this was. It brought back memories that I no longer had the right to think about. Tricia, my expectant wife, was waiting for me in the hotel to take her to breakfast.

"You are an idiot!" My wife should be with me, or I should be with her. How was this marriage going to work if we didn't even want to sleep together on vacation? This island was paradise, and I was standing inside the suite of a woman who put crazy wicked ideas and desires in my head from the moment I first saw her and continued to do so. Something had to change.

I crushed the panties in my hand and carried them and her dress into the bedroom. She was no longer lying in bed, so I took them into the bathroom intending to hang her dress on the hook behind the door, and instead saw the sun streaming in the window behind Merci outlining her incredible body. The same body that both Jameron and I had witnessed earlier shivering under a stream of icy water. The unreasonable feelings of jealousy that hit me were utterly unexpected. Jameron had stood there next to me and watched my Merci in all her glory. The clear image of her perfect breasts, tiny waist, and clean-shaven mound would be forever burned in my mind, and probably his as well.

The water had stopped running, and I don't know how long I stood there staring.

Then Merci, standing naked dripping wet for the second time today, asked, "Could you hand me a towel?"

I pulled it off the rack and threw it at her, then turned and ran out of the bedroom and out the front door as fast as I could.

Merci

Opening the shower and finding Ryan standing there staring at me had been a surprise, but seeing the hungry look in his eyes had been an even bigger shock. He still wanted me and knowing that confused me. His mixed signals and messages were not what I needed. I was trying to move on with my life. He told me himself while lying next to me that he had to let me go because he was going to be a father.

He was going to be a father. That is what I must focus on; I wasn't going to be a homewrecker. I didn't need a man in my life. I didn't need one, but I sure wanted one. I still wasn't sure why he was meeting my boss for breakfast, but I decided I could play this game of his just as good as he could.

I wasn't going to be a homewrecker, and I would make sure he understood that there was other fish to fry in the sea, and I was going to fry them up in front of him.

I quickly got dressed, then I put some moose in my hair and finger combed through it to make the curls pop on their own. My makeup was still in the other room, and I wasn't going there yet, but I did have some lipstick and lip gloss in my purse and a small bottle of perfume. I would go aux natural, make up free, and look the part of miss sweet and innocent. Ryan would find out that I was over him completely and I would start working on my plan to prove it to him during breakfast. *Now if I could only convince myself that I was truly over him.*

I locked the door to my suite, then made my way to the beach. It was only a few minutes central hotel from here, and I knew I wouldn't have any problems finding the restaurant. The smell of food trickling out was calling to me.

There it was in front of me. I was late, but I would explain to Troy later what had kept me. Only the part about the snake. Actually, that would have included both Jameron and Ryan, so I guess I would have to forego the snake story too.

The girl standing at the counter near the front door of the restaurant seemed bored when she asked me if I needed a table for one.

"I'm meeting someone inside; I believe you know Jameron?"

Her attitude changed instantly. "Oh, I'm sorry to have kept you waiting, miss. Please follow me." I guess knowing the person who ran the resort gave me bonus points.

I followed her through the restaurant and saw the table of hot men sitting by a big picture window, with a spectacular view of the beach and ocean. Jameron saw me first and stood up. Both Ryan and Troy followed his lead when they saw me coming.

Jameron took my hand, "Miss Lachance, you look radiant this morning. Sleeping on the beach agrees with you." He kissed my knuckles then pulled out the seat next to him for me to sit down.

Thank you, Jameron. "Thank you so much for your kind words. I don't feel so radiant this morning. In fact, I might want to change my accommodations and move to the main hotel." I picked up the menu next to me.

Troy was the first one to speak after my statement. "I told you last night, Merci, that the top floor was the place to be. Jameron told me you had a small snake problem this morning."

"He did? It was…"

"It was a small snake, but it will not happen again. Merci, I can assure you of that. I do believe you would enjoy the beach accommodations more than being inside the hotel. Please reconsider, you can always call for my assistance should you need help again."

He was trying to save face for both me and Ryan. "Thank you, Jameron. I don't know what I would have done if you hadn't been in calling distance earlier. I will consider your offer."

I gave him a dazzling smile to show him my appreciation. "Can you suggest something for breakfast, I am starving after all the excitement I had this morning."

I glanced at Ryan quickly before focusing on my boss. "Troy, you know my tastes, what would you suggest?" They all started making suggestions to me.

Our server arrived at the table with their food. She put everything down before asking if there was anything else that they needed, then she focused on me. "What can I get you, Miss?"

"First, bring me a small orange juice and a cup of coffee while I decide. Thank you." I was already having a blast. Ryan still hadn't said a word to me, and Jameron was so attentive. Even Troy seemed to be trying harder to please me.

Not one of them had started eating. I giggled, "Please don't wait for me. For heaven's sake. I won't be responsible for cold food, not at these prices." Ryan started choking on a mouthful of liquid.

I looked around the table at the different plates of food. "What are you having, Jameron?"

"It is Eggs Benedict, a specialty of the kitchen with some fresh fruit."

The server brought me my coffee and juice. "I will have the Eggs Benedict and fruit plate, please."

Then Ryan spoke. "Do you think the prices are too high?"

Ryan

When I saw Merci approach the table, I just about shit my pants. She had probably walked right past Tricia. My wife had decided she didn't feel well and had asked to be excused when I arrived for breakfast. She was sitting at the table with Troy and Jameron chatting away. I did notice that she had almost finished her omelet.

Tricia wasn't much older than Merci, but she could have never pulled off going without makeup. Merci on the other hand did; her skin was flawless, and she didn't have the wear and tear on her skin that overdrinking, and smoking had put on the women who I was married too. I knew first hand that Merci was almost a virgin when it came to alcohol. She wasn't a smoker either.

Hearing her remark about the prices made me think. She was more in the average household income bracket. If she thought things were too expensive, then others would too. I was surprised at how much she had changed my thinking. I'd been a rich snob before meeting her, and just recently I found it essential to change other people's opinions of me.

"Do you think the prices are too high? I'm serious? What would you consider a fair price for that plate of food?"

I watched her roll her lips back and forth between her teeth, then she finally answered. "Not that I could ever afford to go here on my own, but if I ever did, I would hope that I could afford to feed my family and still have money left over to pay for other things. I'm sure the prices here are close to what the other resorts are charging. So besides the beach location, what else would draw someone here if they were staying elsewhere and what would make them choose this location over the one they chose to begin with? I only arrived last night, and I don't know what this property has to offer, but the food should be both affordable and exceptional."

Troy spoke next. "And that is why I brought Merci with me on this trip. She's an average, woman, who knows what the average person wants, and she has brilliant ideas on how to change things." It was silent after he said that.

I couldn't stop myself from saying, "Oh, you are quite wrong about that, Troy. There is nothing average about Merci."

Chapter Eight

Ryan

We were all sitting outside at the beach bar testing some of Sam's newest concoctions. "We are lucky to have you here, Merci. Your insight into the minds of women has been constructive, don't you think so, West?"

Merci still hadn't figured out who I was, and it was probably impossible to keep that information from her any longer. "It was beneficial. Thank you, Merci. Wait, what has Jameron been calling you? I thought your last name was Crandall." She peeked up at me and dazzled me with her smile. Not only me but I noticed that Jameron seemed quite taken with her as well.

"I mentioned to Jameron earlier that I wanted to take my maiden name back now that I'm divorced. My name was Merci Rose Lachance. I intend to have it officially changed back to that as soon as I return home."

"That's a beautiful name; it fits you."

"Thank you, Ryan. I thought about doing it before, but worried how it might affect my girls. After hearing my name rolling off Jameron's tongue, I made a firm decision. Thank you for your encouragement, Jameron."

Her interaction with my general manager was starting to piss me off. "Jameron when you are finished flirting with Miss Lachance, I need you to get started on the project we discussed earlier."

Merci gave me a puzzled look then asked, "What right do you have to order him around, Ryan. He wasn't flirting; we were talking. I'm sorry, Jameron, I haven't seen this side of him before."

"It's quite all right, Merci, after all, he is my boss."

Well now the cat was out of the bag, and Merci looked even more puzzled than she had before. "What do you mean, he is your boss? I thought Mr. Masters had me come with him on this trip to do business for Western Wind Resorts. Isn't that you, Jameron?"

I had to say something to her before she turned the whole cat loose. Troy was enjoying the entire exchange between us; I knew he was waiting for an opportunity to stick it to me somehow. "Merci, I should have said something to you when we first met. Yes, I own Western Wind Resorts and all the properties associated with it. I'm Ryan West."

I watched her face to see if she had made the connection yet. She had, and her entire face went through different emotions all at once. I didn't like the one it landed on when she stared at me.

"You made a fool out of me, Mr. West. I don't appreciate that at all." She looked at Troy and then at Jameron. They were both aware that I had known Merci before she was brought here, but they didn't know to what extent. She could ruin my reputation if they found out, Troy in particular.

"I hope you all enjoyed your little game at my expense." I watched her eyes fill with tears. "I don't even have a safe room to go back to, and I can't afford a plane back home." She got up from her bar stool, then turned and started down the beach. Jameron stood up and followed her.

"That was entertaining. How do you know her, West? I knew you two had met before from the way you reacted to her when I ran into you the other day in the parking lot of *The Surrender*. Has Patricia met her?"

I picked up my drink and swallowed down the contents before I looked at him. "Yes, she has. I have a question for you. When did you start calling my wife, Patricia?"

Merci

I didn't know where I was going to go. I felt betrayed and used by both Troy and Ryan. Was this all a game to them? See how many young gullible women you can bag then dump them to head off into the happily ever after with your pregnant wife? I hadn't even grabbed a napkin to wipe my runny nose.

I stopped and picked up the bottom of my dress to wipe my face, and that's when I heard Jameron calling my name.

"Merci, slow down girl. Please wait for me. I'm not your enemy, only a friend."

I finished wiping my face, then felt his warm hand on my shoulder. "How do I know you aren't like the other two? I want to go h…home to my girls." I started crying again and felt his warm arms circle me. He began to rock back and forth as we stood together in the sand.

"Hush, Merci. Ma chère enfant ne pleure pas."

"I am not a child, Jameron. I'm a grown woman with really hurt feelings, and I'm afraid to go to my suite filled with snakes." I spoke into his chest, then took in a deep breath. Jameron's smell was woodsy and clean. It was so different than Ryan's had been earlier today.

"I know very well that you are a fully-grown woman, Merci. I saw all that you had to offer, and you are a beautiful woman."

I didn't need to be reminded of that and tried to twist free from his arms. "Stop moving, ma petite fille. I am ashamed to have brought that up; will you please forgive me?"

"I don't know what I'm going to do, but I will forgive you only if you come with me and check my rooms to make sure there are no snakes in them. Especially the overly large ones that want to squeeze the life out of me, and I'm talking reptile, not Ryan and Troy."

Jameron tossed his head back, and his laughter was contagious. I felt myself start to smile, then eventually I was laughing along with him.

He still had his arms around me, but it felt safe. I trusted Jameron Sebastián; he wouldn't hurt me. "Will you come with me just to make sure there are no more wild beasts in my suite, either that or find me somewhere else to go, I don't' even want to be in the hotel knowing what my boss and your boss are probably up to."

"Come, Merci. I will prove to you that you are safe. I have something else to show you as well."

Jameron took my small hand in his larger one, and we walked back to my suite. "Do you have your keys, Merci?"

"Oh patootie, I left my purse at the bar with Ryan. That's just flippin great now isn't it?"

Jameron tossed his head back and laughed once again. "Merci, you bring sunshine into my dreary world. I have the master keys, but let me phone the bar and have Sam, put your purse in his safe for safe keeping."

"Ha, no pun intended, right?"

Jameron pulled the two-way radio from his belt and called Sam to explain to him what had happened. "Please be discreet, don't alert Mr. West, I will take care of this for the lady. Thank you, Sam. Done, Merci. We can pick it up in the morning unless there is something that you need from it tonight. In that case, I will go and bring it back to you now."

"No!" I said the word louder than I had intended too. I didn't want him leaving me without first checking to make sure my room was safe. "Maybe I should stay inside the hotel, after all, I don't know if I can do this."

"We are here, and I will stay with you until you feel safe again. I want to show you what has been done to fix the problem."

He opened the door to my suite, and I noticed right away that it had been cleaned. He grabbed onto my hand and almost pulled me behind him. "Look, Miss Lachance. There will be no more beasts surprising you in your shower."

I didn't want to step foot in that bathroom again, but he went inside and encouraged me to follow. "We have snake traps and heavy-duty netting installed in all of the suites on the beach. Look for yourself, Merci."

Stretched across the top of the shower was a heavy-duty net, and on the top of all the edges were one-inch metal spikes which stood straight up. "Should a snake decide to try his luck in the shower, the spikes will scratch his underbelly. This was the first time that a snake has ever been reported to us before in one of the showers, and it will be the last time, Merci. You are safe, and I understand you may not want to use the facility again, but I hope this will put your mind at ease."

Ryan

My plans had changed for the evening. I had really enjoyed my day listening to Merci's ideas. She was a pistol, full of valid, useful information. Troy had been right about that; having a woman's input had been very valuable. Especially someone who had lived on a budget her whole life.

My experiences growing up had always been on the silver spoon side of living. My resorts did tend to cater to the wealthier clients, but why not offer more services to those in Merci's situation who couldn't afford to spend as much while on vacation. I would have my marketing department meet with her when she was ready and go over some ideas to expand my resorts and include some deals which would bring more of the working class to my properties.

I hadn't heard back from Jameron yet. I hoped he stayed with Merci until she felt comfortable in her suite. I didn't want her to sleep anywhere but next to me at night. Troy Masters was up to no good. I could feel it in my bones. He had just laughed in my face when I asked him about Patricia.

Speaking of Patricia, I hadn't seen her all day. I should probably check in with her and find out if she would like to have dinner with me. I still sat at the bar, so asked Sam if I could have the courtesy phone to call her.

"Thank you, Sam. Get me another one of these too please." I held my empty glass up for him.

"Right away, Mr. West."

The phone rang and rang with no answer. I hung it up and tried again. Finally, Tricia picked it up. "Tricia, did I wake you?"

Right away she sounded annoyed; I had disturbed her massage. "Jesus Christ, Tricia, are you ever planning on leaving that room? I thought we were going to work on our marriage while we were here. Reconnect is how you put it." I listened to more of her whining before I responded. "Maybe I can spend the night with you. I can order something special for dinner, and we can sit outside on the balcony and watch the ocean together."

She continued to make excuses, and I'd had enough. "Fine, enjoy your massage, I won't bother you again. When you are ready to resume our marriage, then call me." I slammed the phone down just as Sam set another drink down on the smooth bar top.

This one tasted a bit different than the last one had. "I like this one better than the last. What's in it?"

"It's called *Breakfast in Bed*, It's Fireball Whiskey, butterscotch schnapps, and orange juice. I added some Cherry juice. We could call it *Breakfast on the Beach*."

"I like your thinking, Sam." I'd been drinking most of the day one way or another, and I knew someone who I wanted to serve this to. "I'll have another one when I'm finished with it; it looks like I could be sleeping here tonight. What time do you close?"

"On the weekdays I close at eleven, but I will stay here for as long as you need me to, Mr. West."

The nightly entertainment was setting up on the small stage near the beach. I watched a group of women step out on the sand in front of them to wait for the music to start. Most of them weren't worth looking at, but there was one of them that might be entertaining to watch in her inebriated state of mind. Even better, she looked nothing like Tricia or Merci.

"Sam, let's see what the rest of the night has to offer. It looks like the show is ready to start."

Merci

"Jameron, tell me more about yourself. What made you go to America, to begin with? There can't be anywhere in the states that can compare to Jamaica." I put on some comfortable pajamas while he went to the restaurant to get us food. We were sitting outside on the patio by candlelight eating. I hadn't wanted to, but he insisted. I'm sure it was to prove to me that I was safe from snakes. It had worked for now.

"It is always a woman who makes men do crazy things, Merci."

"What was her name? and what did she look like?"

"Her name was Lucy Victoria. She was beautiful; her skin was like smooth white chocolate. Brown eyes, and a big smile. I followed her to New Orleans. It was hard to find decent work there, for her and me. We both tried for many months. She gave up and became a prostitute. She broke my heart, and I came back here to work for my friend, Ryan."

"A prostitute? How did you find that out? Gosh, I'm so sorry, Jameron."

"I let her down; it was my fault for pushing her so hard to find a good job. I went for a job interview inside a nicer hotel, and she was in the lobby with a client. At least she was doing business in that establishment and not some of the others that I saw while I was there. Enough talk of Lucy. Merci, you make me say things that I haven't said to anyone except for Mr. West."

"You really do care about him, don't you?"

"He offered me the job here and paid off my debt without asking me any questions. He is a good man, Merci. Do you want to tell me how you know him?"

"I can't talk about it; it still hurts too much. But yeah, you are right, I know sure do know him."

We sat there together in silence for a few minutes. "Merci, be careful with him. He is a good man, but he is protective of what is his. He is also a married man with a baby coming soon, and he won't let anyone hurt what is his, even you."

"I've moved on already, Jameron. I was just as surprised to see him here as he was to see me. Yes, I do have very strong feelings for him, but I won't do anything to take that child from its father. My girls don't have theirs in their lives, not by my choice but by his."

Jameron spoke again, and his words sent the goosebumps rolling across my skin. "Do you want me to help you forget about him, Merci?"

Ryan

I tried hard to forget about Merci and Tricia by drowning them in my drink. I lost track of how many of the Breakfast on the Beaches I had, then I finished off the night drinking bourbon straight. Sam had closed the bar on time; I suppose he figured I'd had enough to drink as well.

"Ugh, shoot me now. It would be less painful than trying to walk back to my suite in this fucking sand." At least I had a master key in my possession, so I wouldn't have to figure out which card was mine. I also would be able to use it to enter Tricia's room, but I hadn't wanted to yet.

I could see both my suite ahead and Merci's. Her patio was lit up by candlelight. It would be so easy to stop by and see how she was doing. I stumbled closer to her front door and was getting ready to knock when I heard her laughter mingled with deeper males.

Was that Jameron? Piss on her, and on Tricia. I didn't want the couple to see me walking past their cozy gathering, but trying to find my way through the trees might be worse.

Screw it! I would do this like a man. I walked down and got as near to the water as I could and continued to walk. If they noticed me I would stop to talk, if they didn't, I'd make my way to my room and feel sorry for myself.

"Mr. West, are you all right, sir?"

"Ryan, is that you?"

Oh, bloody hell. I stopped walking and went back toward the patio. "Is it me, am I inerruptin something?"

"Do you need my assistance to help you get back to your room, Ryan?"

"I'm good, Jam. You jes keep helping the lady with her snakes, and I'll see you in the morning. No more drinkin breakfast on the beach. G'night, Jam. G'night, Merci Rose. G'night, snake."

I continued to walk past them both but soon felt Jameron's hand on my shoulder. "Let me assist you, Ryan. I think you had more to drink than you should have. I don't want you falling into the ocean."

"Would it be so wrong if I did? Drown my sorrows the right way now woulden it? Thanks, Jam." I called out to Merci. "I'll have him back to you before you know he's gone, Merci. Don't wait up."

I heard an angel's voice call out to me, "Good night, Ryan. Sleep well."

Chapter Nine

Ryan

What in God's name was that noise? "Go away!" I pulled my pillow over my head but could still hear the pounding coming from the front door.

"This had bloody well be important!" I climbed out of bed and stopped for a moment to let the room catch up with me. Then I slowly made my way to the front door and threw it open. "What do you want?"

Jameron stood outside the door, and I behind him I noticed a group of women walking along the beach. They looked my direction and giggled. "What do you find so fucking hilarious this time of the day?"

"Ryan, you might want to put some pants on next time you answer the door. Can I come inside?"

"Only if you know how to make coffee. I'm not putting on pants until I get some strong black coffee and a bottle of ibuprofen. What in the hell hit me last night?"

"If I remember correctly, you said you drank too much *Breakfast on the beach*. I imagine Sam kept feeding you drinks. I will have a talk with him later about that. Sit down, Ryan, before I must pick you up off the floor. As soon as you get your coffee, I will help you into the shower. You do know you missed breakfast, and it is almost lunchtime?"

Jameron continued to punish me while I sat on the couch trying to remember what had made me drink so much. "Did you sleep with Merci?"

Jameron stopped his movements and stood still. "And if I had is it any of your business?"

"You slept with her? I knew it. Get out of my sight before I…I."

"I did not sleep with the girl. Sit back down and listen to me before you do or say something you might regret. Ryan, you are a married man, and you and your wife are expecting a child. You told me yourself that you were trying to make your marriage work. If this is true, why do you still worry about that beautiful girl who is staying next door?"

I scrubbed my hands up and down across my face. "I know you are right, but when I can't get my wife or my dick to cooperate, then what am I supposed to do?"

Jameron handed me a cup of coffee. "That is hot; I will return with your medicine. Don't burn yourself while I am away."

"Very funny, Jam. I'm not a child."

"Then quit acting like one. Be the man I have known for most of my life, Ryan. You will only hurt that girl if you continue this way. Move into the hotel and be with your wife."

"Why, so you can take my place next to Merci?"

"Your place isn't next to Merci." He handed me four ibuprofens, and I swallowed them down with the hot coffee.

"Son of a bitch, that coffee is hot! Why didn't you warn me?"

"I'm warning you now, Ryan. Leave that sweet thing alone and move in with your wife."

"So that's how it's going to be now is it?"

"I love you, Ryan. You are a good man. Do the right thing for everyone. Merci is a beautiful young woman who still hasn't found Mr. Right. Don't take that opportunity away from her. He could be knocking at her door very soon."

I laughed out loud. "Ha, and now you are a philosopher? I'm sorry, Jameron. I've been an ass, and I have no right coming down on you. Sorry, man. I guess drowning my sorrows last night didn't do anything to help my situation. Did you meet Troy for breakfast?"

"Yes, he was there and so was your wife and Merci. When he asked where you were, I told him you were taking care of other resort business. He is expecting to see you in your office at two. Tricia is lying by the pool and Merci is on the beach. Get in the shower while I order you some food."

Merci

I finally had some beach time. I hadn't spent all this money on bikinis to have them waste away in my wardrobe bag. Jameron told me He would check on Ryan and make sure he was okay. I knew Ryan was in bad shape when I saw him late last night. He sounded completely wasted. Jameron explained that Sam had let him try some of the new Beach themed drinks they were going to use in the bar. He had over indulged.

Jameron. The man made me smile. He had stayed in the spare bedroom with me, sitting in the chair just in case I had nightmares. Which I had more than once. The last one had involved snakes hidden in candy jars, and wooden men trying to jump and land on them. It was horrible. I convinced him to sleep on top of the sheets with me. He was a complete gentleman and had done just that, which left me a little peeved.

I knew he was single, and he knew that I was. Why was he holding back? Oh, Well. I still had twelve more days to work on him. I would do anything to make sure that I stopped thinking about Ryan.

I had on my skimpiest bikini. I'd get the smallest tan lines in the beginning so no matter what else I wore; the lines wouldn't interfere. I had found a nice quiet spot a little way down from the bar. I had been the only one here when I first arrived. Now there was a few couples and a family, but other than that, I was all alone. Which also gave me, even more, time to think.

At breakfast, I had the pleasure of dining with Ryan's wife, Troy, and Jameron. She hadn't remembered me at all, which was a good thing. Jameron had focused on me the entire time, and Troy had flirted with Patricia. Actually, it had sounded like they were both flirting with each other. In fact, I had seen them at the hotel pool together on my way here. Poor Ryan, I knew he had asked her to join him yesterday. She must be getting over her initial morning sickness and was feeling better. I was more than happy that she was keeping Troy out of my hair.

I sat up on my elbows and looked around. The beach had a few more people on it now, and I saw a bunch of younger men putting up a net on the beach to play volleyball. They were all quite hunky, and much too young for me, but I would definitely enjoy myself watching them put on a show.

I was getting warm and stood up and hurried into the ocean to cool off. On my way back to my towel a few of the volleyball hunks whistled at me. I called out to them, "I'm old enough to be someone's mother."

"You can adopt me." And other responses were volleyed back and forth between the group of them.

"Funny, you look a little too old to baby."

"Then don't baby me. Hey, do you play volleyball?"

"I haven't played it since I was in high school."

"That was when, last year?" There was one boy in the group in particular who kept the conversation going. He was muscular, blond, and full of himself, but he sure did have a charming smile.

I decided it was time to have some fun with the boys. Why not, I was old enough to know better, even if they weren't, but they didn't know a thing about me. "I'll play if you put me up front."

Ryan

I finally got my head and my emotions under control thanks to Jameron. "Do you think Tricia is still at the pool? I wanted her to join me there yesterday, but she didn't feel well."

"It doesn't hurt to try, my friend. She can only say no. Get dressed, and I will escort you back. I should check on Merci and make sure she hasn't gotten herself lost."

We got to the pool just as Tricia was getting ready to go back inside. She had a beach cover on, and her cheeks were just a little pink. "Are you leaving already? I wanted to swim with you."

Tricia smiled at me. "I've had too much sun already. Troy left for the beach. Apparently, there is some kind of a volleyball game going on that's drawing a crowd. Why don't you go and check it out? I'm going to take a nap." She leaned over and barely kissed my cheek. "Later, Ry."

"Oh, well. I got more from her today than I did yesterday. Jam, are you up for some volleyball? Hey, did you schedule a game for this week?"

"No, but whoever is playing is good for business. Look at all the customers lined up at the bar. Let's see for ourselves what is going on; maybe we will find Merci in the crowd."

We followed the cocktail totting group to the beach. We couldn't see who was playing, only the cheers when somebody scored. Jameron stayed close to my side as we pushed our way through the crowd to see what was going on.

I heard Jameron say over the din of the crowd as my mouth dropped open. "No wonder they are so thirsty, can you see who is playing?"

"Merci?" There she was bouncing around in the sand in all her glory wearing almost nothing. The turquoise blue string bikini wasn't made to contain that body and would have been classified as scanty even had she just been lying quietly on the beach. But Jameron was correct; she was bringing us a lot of thirsty customers, male ones mostly, and she was having fun.

"She is a beautiful girl, Ryan."

"I'll agree with you on that one."

I'm sure every male in the crowd was hoping she'd fall out of her top, or that she'd break a string reaching for the ball, but her suit held up to all the activity she put it through. The game ended, and I started forward to say something to her but was stopped when a young, blond, god picked her up from the sand and spun her around in the air.

He covered her mouth with his, and Jameron grabbed onto my shoulder to stop me from moving forward. "Just wait, my friend. If she wants his attention, then let her have it. Wait and see what she will do before you go in there to rescue the girl who you must forget."

I shrugged off his hand and waited. Merci let him finish his kiss, then pushed herself out of his arms and thanked him for the fun morning. I saw more than one male adjust himself when they were through; I included.

Merci turned and noticed Jameron and me standing there watching her and grinned. "Did you see me kick their young butts?"

Jameron spoke, I was still too tongue-tied to speak straight. "Yes, I did, Merci. You must get out of the sun now. You are going to be sunburned, and tomorrow you won't have anything to show for it but peeling skin. Let me help you gather your things. Do you have something to put on over your suit?"

"What suit, she is wearing nothing but string."

"Did you say something to me, Ryan?"

"Nope, get dressed, Merci. I will see you in my office at two; It's a quarter till, so you had better make it fast."

Merci

I watched Ryan turn around and walk back toward his hotel. He walked as if he had an iron rod stuck up his butt, and I wondered who had put it there. "Jameron, I just can't figure that man out."

I loved his honeyed laughter. "Merci, don't even try. You were very good for business today. The beach bar was booming earlier. You never told me you could play volleyball."

"I haven't played since I was in high school. That was a lot of fun, but I can feel my skin burning now. Do you think I have time to change my clothes? I need to get some aloe vera on my skin soon."

I will come with you; my hands will cover more skin quicker than your small ones will." He picked up my hand and turned it over to kiss the palm. "Do you trust me, Merci?"

"Absolutely, Jameron. Do you trust me?"

"We will see what happens later. Come, we must hurry."

We raced back to my suit, and I felt giddy and powerful. I had seen the look in Ryan's eyes and Jameron's. It was a heady feeling. We only had a few minutes, but I was turned on by all the attention I had gotten on the beach. I wondered how far I could push Jameron before he would break.

"I'm going to shower with cold water quickly to cool my skin down. Will you wait for me?"

"Of, course, Merci. Hurry or my boss will have my head."

I jumped into the shower in the spare bedroom; it would be a while before I could go back into the other one. I rinsed myself off quickly, and I could already see how pink some areas of my skin were turning. I hurried out of the shower and wrapped myself in the towel, then I picked up the aloe vera and walked into the living room and stood in front of Jameron.

I had done something this brazen only once before, and it was the last time I had gone to Ryan's suite with him. I handed Jameron the bottle of lotion, then turned around to put my back toward him.

"Could you help me put some lotion on?" I let the towel drop and heard his quick intake of breath.

"Merci, you are a witch, and I have fallen under your spell, but I won't do something that we could both regret at another time." He picked up my towel and handed it back to me. "Cover yourself; then I will put lotion on your back."

I felt so foolish but did as he asked, then I took the towel and covered myself up. He kissed the side of my neck softly before he squeezed the lotion into his hands, then rubbed the cool substance over the top of my back.

"I know what you think you want for me, but I can't do that until I know you are sure. Get dressed, Merci." He turned and walked away from me.

"I will wait outside for you to finish." I heard the door shut, and I took a few minutes to get my breathing under control.

"Oh, Lordy." What in the world had gotten into me? He was right; I didn't know if he is what I wanted. I was foolish, but thankfully he was thinking about the consequences; I sure hadn't been.

I hurried back into the bedroom and slipped into one of my new sundresses and tied it behind my neck. I put on a pair of thong undies, then ran a brush through my hair. I loved going without makeup; it saved a lot of time, and it didn't melt all over my face in the sun. I applied my lipstick and gloss, then grabbed my sandals and went outside to meet Jameron.

Chapter Ten

Ryan

"We will wait just a few more minutes for Merci and Jameron before we begin.

"Did you happen to see Merci out on the beach playing volleyball earlier. Man oh, man. I sure wished I wasn't her boss; I could tap…"

I reached over and grabbed him by the neck with my right hand and threw him up against the wall. "Don't you ever speak of her that way again. Do you hear me, Masters? She is not anyone's plaything, and that includes you and me both." I let go of him and straightened my shirt as I walked away from him.

"Woah there, you sound like you are jealous. Isn't your wife upstairs in a room all by herself. I'd be worried about her before you get all over someone else's shit because of a secretary. Christ man, get a hold of yourself." Then he started laughing. "I get it now; you've been banging her yourself haven't you. That's priceless."

"Knock it off, Masters. I said knock it off. It's none of your business what I've been doing."

"Wow, I sure made that convenient for you, didn't I. Here I thought I'd bring little miss Merci along for some laughs and instead I made it easier for you to get to her. She's right next to you on the beach."

Troy walked around the room picking up different objects and muttering to himself. "What is it now, Masters? What do you want from me?"

"I want you to give me back what is rightfully mine." Troy stopped in front of me and tapped my desk with the end of a pencil.

"And what is that?"

Just then we heard a knocking on the door, and Jameron walked into the room with Merci following him from behind.

"Merci, I caught your show on the beach. Why didn't you tell me before how well you could play volleyball?"

Her already pink tinted cheeks deepened into a blush. "I played on the girls' volleyball team in high school. I had forgotten how much fun it had been. It was quite a workout."

"For all of us." Troy's comment had been said just loud enough for us all to hear.

"That was an unnecessary remark, Masters. Get off your high horse and act like the gentleman you are supposed to be. Merci, you were good for business; I just wished that I had the energy that you do." I focused on Troy when I spoke, "Gentlemen, shall we continue with the tour of the facilities?"

We had discussed the restaurant and the beach café the day before; today we were going to look for ways to improve the rooms. The suites needed updating, as well as the laundry, maintenance, garage and the front desk and reception area.

Jameron had a list of the unoccupied rooms; we were starting with the most affordable rooms and working our way up to the penthouse suites. "Merci, I really appreciated the suggestions you had for us yesterday. Please feel free to offer your opinion today. Let me get you a pencil and notebook. Jot down any ideas that you might have, and we can discuss them afterward unless something catches your eye right away. Jameron, lead the way."

"Merci, after you. Make your way to the elevators. We will start on the second floor. How is Tricia feeling this afternoon, Ryan?" Jameron was polite when he asked me the question.

"She is a little on the overdone side. But at least she left her room. She promised me dinner later on tonight."

Merci

All three of them were gentlemen during the tour. Whatever Troy and Ryan had been discussing before Jameron and I entered the room must have been forgotten. They joked around and kidded with Jameron and me during the tour. I enjoyed all their company, and they made me feel like I was valuable. I did have many suggestions to tell them about, but nothing that couldn't wait to be discussed until later. I made notes on every room that we went into.

We had reached the floor that Troy was staying on. "Why don't we go into my room and order room service. We can have a drink and converse over things while they are still fresh in our minds."

"Yay, and I can use the bathroom."

We followed Troy into his room, and the layout reminded me of the one that Ryan and I had stayed in. "Ryan, this is just like the one that..." I realized my mistake when Troy began laughing. "I'm sorry, Ryan, I didn't mean to say that."

Troy stood in the middle of the room grinning at the two of us. "Isn't this cozy. I can think of one thing that needs changing immediately. I'm sure you can too, West."

"What is that supposed to mean?" Ryan moved over to stand face to face with my boss.

"I'd say all of your suites need updating if one looks the same as another. Don't you think the ones in paradise should be a bit more unique than the ones you take your friends to back home?"

Jameron said loud enough that both men could hear him. "Mr. Masters, if you would like me to find you different accommodations in another hotel, that could be arranged. You are leaving a bad taste in my mouth, and you are both acting like children, I am sorry, Miss Lachance. I am ashamed and embarrassed by both men who behave without any consideration of your feelings. Would you like to accompany me downstairs? We can relax outside in the café until these two grow up."

I appreciated what Jameron was trying to do. "Thank you for your thoughtful suggestion, but I would like to see how well room service operates at this hotel. I'm going to take a few minutes to tidy up, would someone please order me something refreshing and loaded with ice. I'd like to try one of the new drinks on the menu. The Seaside Sangria sounds delicious."

I made my way to the bathroom, and surprise, surprise. It was just like the one that I had been in inside Ryan's suite. *If it's not broke then don't fix it, right?* The layout of the suite and the bathroom flowed very well. I didn't see any reason to change it. On the other hand, adjusting the color scheme to give it a more tropical appearance was an excellent idea.

I used the bathroom, then washed my hands in the sink. Things sure had deteriorated between Troy and Ryan. What was going on with those two? I wondered if Jameron knew anything. Maybe I could get him to talk more to me later; get him to spill the beans.

I walked out of the bathroom to see they were all playing nicely again. I made my way over to look out the window. "Troy, I believe you told me the views from up here were worth the stay. Can somebody come over here and point the different landmarks out to me?"

Jameron hurried over. "Food is on the way, and we are all going to try the Seaside Sangria." He stepped closer and pointed toward one of the taller mountains. "That is Morne fortune or the hill of good luck. It overlooks the Castries which was a key battleground during the skirmishes over who would take possession of St. Lucia in the seventeen-hundreds. The French started building a fortress there, but it was finished by the British."

"The French? Is there more history in town on the French? I would love to take a trip one day and learn more."

Jameron winked at me. "I know someone who knows someone who might take you. Right boss?"

I wondered if he meant himself, or Ryan. "Tell me more; I had no idea this place was full of so much history." I listened to him talk as he pointed in the different directions that could be seen from this window. Troy was right, the views up here were spectacular, and seeing them through Jameron's eyes was even better.

There was a knock at the door, and someone on the other side of the door called out, 'Room Service.'

Ryan

I enjoyed watching Merci interact with Jameron. She had no idea how beautiful she was when her face lit up at something he was saying. Or how engaging her laughter was when she teased him, and he played along with her.

"She's something else. I think her and Jameron make a good match, what do you think, Ryan?" Troy was baiting me again.

"I think you are right; it couldn't happen to a better man. After he lost, Lucy, I didn't think he would ever be the same. It sounds as if room service has arrived."

I asked the chef in the restaurant to send up some of the new food entries he had come up with that I wanted to use on the new menu. There was a tropical fruit dish with a scoop of both sherbet and cottage cheese, Teriyaki chicken skewers with fresh pineapple, red bell pepper and garlic served with a rice pilaf, and a plate of appetizers. They had sent a large pitcher of the sangria with fruit-filled glasses.

The concierge set everything out on the table, then assisted Merci into her seat before pouring each one of us our drinks. Then he set the plates in front of us and waited to make sure we didn't need anything else from him before he left.

Merci dazzled him with her smile, "This looks delicious. Thank you, Badrick." She caught my eye. "Ryan, I am impressed, the room service is very efficient, quick, and gracious. Badrick, could I please get more ice for my drink?" How could anyone refuse the girl when she asked so nicely.

"I'm glad you are so pleased, Merci. Now I want you to tell me what you think of the new dishes that the chef sent up for us."

We finished every bit of the food, including the appetizers. I didn't care for the Arepas salad with octopus and lobster, but everything else had been fantastic. "Badrick, please feel our glasses one more time, then tell the chef everything was excellent. I will speak with him about the octopus dish later."

He did as I asked, then bowed toward, Merci. She giggled and thanked him again. "Badrick, you've got impeccable manners. Can I bring you home with me, so you can teach them to my girls?"

He was quite flustered by all her attention. "Thank you, Miss. You are very kind, but I must stay in St. Lucia."

"She is paying you a compliment, Badrick. She is not serious about taking you home with her."

Jameron threw his head back and laughed. "Badrick, Miss Merci est une jeune mère qui veut le meilleur pour ses deux petites filles. Elle parle aussi bien Français. She is very beautiful as well."

I didn't like being left out of the conversation, not when it concerned Merci. "Tell us all what you said, Jameron. I only understood a few words."

Badrick looked at me and smiled. "It is hard to believe that she is a mother with girls of her own, Mr. West. Her husband is a lucky man."

Yes, he had been, but I knew better. "Thank you, Badrick, that will be all." We waited for him to finish clearing the table, then I stood up and asked Merci to join me for a moment at a window that had a different view of St. Lucia.

"What is it, Ryan?" She stood close to me, close enough for me to see how flawless her skin was in the sunlight, and I caught just a whiff of the coconut oil that she had rubbed into her skin.

"Look that way. There are miles and miles of sand, and at the very end of the sand is two moss-covered mountains with granite peeking through at the tops. They stand side by side. Do you see them?" I moved over a bit so that she could move closer, then I leaned over her shoulder and pointed them out.

"Yes, I can see them, they are so similar to one another. What are they called, and how far are they from here?

"They are called the St. Lucia Pitons, and it is said they were entered to be listed as the eighth natural wonders of the world. They almost look like twins. You must make sure to see them while you are here."

Jameron walked over to look out the window as well. "They are most impressive from a boat just before dusk. Can I take you there this weekend, Merci, unless you had other plans for her to work, Ryan?"

Merci

"That would be amazing. Could we take a trip to see the Morne of Fortune also?"

Ryan turned away and left us standing at the window. "Knock yourself out. Let's continue with the tour; we still have the penthouse to look at; it's one of three."

Jameron leaned over and whispered in my ear. "Je suis désolé de pied à, Merci. Si yo demanderais plutôt Ryan et sa femme de prendre vous que je comprends."

"Oh, no, Jameron. I wouldn't want to be a third wheel. Thank you for offering to take me though. Ryan, is your wife feeling well enough to make that trip?"

"What are you telling her now, Sebastian? I told you no more French. That reminds me, we need to make this quick, I'm meeting my wife for dinner and dancing, and I've got to have plenty of time to get ready. Jameron, will you please lead the way to the penthouse?"

Ryan did have to go and ruin things for me. I had been the one who had mentioned her. In a voice I didn't recognize as mine, I said, "That sounds lovely, Ryan. Are you going to be dining and dancing here in the hotel with her?"

"As a matter of fact, I am. The entertainment tonight is a popular jazz group from St. Lucia. They are incredible; they usually bring in quite a crowd. Tricia has been dying to see them with me."

I don't know why I had even remembered their name. But I did, and I wanted to hurt him back as much as he had just hurt me. "Are they anything like Dirty Rush, Ryan? Jameron, are you familiar with their music? I recently attended a nightclub where they were playing. They have a popular song out called, Slow Motion. I wonder if the jazz group that is playing here knows that one. Do you like to dance, Jameron?"

"Miss Lachance, dancing is in my blood. I would very much like to take you dancing. When we are in town, I will take you to one of my favorite places to dance. In Jamaica, we have our own style; to have a beautiful woman by my side will make me the envy of all my friends."

Just hearing the enthusiasm in his voice when he spoke of his blessed Jamaica, and the traditions of his country had me excited to spend more time with him. "I am one lucky woman then. It is a date."

It could have been my imagination, but it seemed that Ryan was short tempered. He glared at us both. "Can we finish this conversation in the elevator?"

"I apologize Mr. West. Follow me."

We went over many things in the penthouse. It was probably the room that needed most updating than any of the others we had seen. I had to know why. "Ryan, I'm sure these are the most expensive rooms in your hotel, so why are they the most outdated? Shouldn't these rooms be more luxurious than the rest? I don't understand why you haven't put the money into them that you have everywhere else."

"I'll tell you why Merci. We don't rent these out as much as we do the other rooms, the cost to stay in one is twice as much per night as the deluxe suites are."

"Then wouldn't it make sense to make everything in them the top of the line and promote them more? For instance, offer a getaway package, in the penthouse with a view, and include a spa package, or include a candlelight dinner and entertainment. There are so many things that could draw a crowd if you offer the right amenities."

Troy responded to my suggestion with one of his own. "I like your thinking, Merci. How much money did you want to go into this renovation, to begin with? If you are going to do it, do it big or go home. I think Merci is on to something here. I've stayed at another resort nearby, and they don't have a penthouse at all. Your hotel is situated on the beach, and you can see the twins from up here as well as views of the ocean, and the beach. Marketing, renovations, and someone with Merci's virgin excitement could do wonders for your resort."

"That is a silly thing to say; I'm not a virgin, Troy."

"It's a figure of speech, Merci. Fresh, uncorrupted, that's all I meant. What do you think, Ryan?"

"We've got a lot to do in a short amount of time. When are you going back home, Troy?"

Chapter Eleven

Ryan

By the time we had left our tour of the penthouse, I was pissed off at all three of them. During the ride down in the elevator, Merci and Jam had talked about music. But it was probably Merci's suggestion that Jameron take her dancing with him in the restaurant tonight that had made me the maddest. I knew he was attracted to Merci, and she seemed to feel the same about him.

I couldn't get out of the elevator and away from their happy chatter fast enough. Why did I care how they felt about each other? I should give them my blessings and get on with my life.

"Fuck my life!" All I knew was I had better do something to turn my marriage around tonight, or Tricia and I might not make it back to our happy place. I hurried down the beach and focused on how I would make my wife happy to be with me. If she wanted me to spend the night with her in her room, then I would do anything to make that happen for us. I just had to convince myself that was what I wanted, and stick to my guns.

I reached my suite and removed my clothing as I made my way to the bathroom. I needed a long hot shower to wash away all the aggravation that being close to Merci had caused me.

I turned on the shower and glanced up. I was happy to see the snake traps had been installed immediately. We had made sure that the snake episode wouldn't happen again. Merci's incident had been a fluke, but I was relieved that I had been nearby when it had happened. I still didn't want to think about what might have occurred if Jam and I hadn't been on that beach just at the right moment.

I turned the taps to the hottest setting before stepping into the shower. I was alone; nothing was stopping me from fantasizing about the girl who had caught my interest from the moment I first saw her. I took my time in the shower; I thought back to the night we spent together, and how much she had changed since then. Merci shivering in the shower, her breasts heaving as she breathed hard in fear. Merci on the beach playing volleyball, every male waiting, hoping for a strap to give out and expose her perfect tits. It didn't take me long to slake my needs with her on my mind.

As soon as I finished dressing, I called up Tricia to make sure she was still up for our night of dining and dancing. "Wear something sexy for me; I want to make love to my wife tonight. I will see you soon, Tricia."

I needed to seduce my wife, but the memory of Merci's body was still whirling through my thoughts. Oh well, what Tricia didn't know wouldn't hurt her. I took my time as I walked along the beach. I loved this place, and I'd do anything to stay here forever. Maybe I'd use that approach tonight with Tricia. I knew she liked it here too, but could she give up her friends and the nightlife back home?

I had on a nice pair of slacks, and a short-sleeved linen shirt. I'd let my hair grow longer than It had been for a while. I had a few days growth on my face, Tricia didn't like facial hair, but I hoped to convince her to let me keep it. I knew it felt good scrapping against her skin. Or had that been on Merci's skin? I shook my head; I needed a drink before I went up to Tricia's suite. I sat down at the beach bar and asked Sam to surprise me with another one of his specials.

"I call this one, *'Better than Sex on the Beach'.* Take a big swallow the first time you taste it."

"This had better be good because I can't think of anything that could be better than that." I did as he asked and took a big gulp. "That wasn't bad. Tell me, what is different than your typical *'Sex on the beach'*, cocktail?" I took another large sip and rolled it in my mouth.

"It has the usual ingredients. Vodka, peach schnapps, crème de cassis, OJ, cranberry juice, and fresh cherries. I add a shot of rum and champagne. Hang on, boss. In just a minute you will see what I mean, it packs quite a punch."

He wasn't kidding, it was similar to a Long Island ice tea, but the fruit juices hid the alcohol taste. "I like it, a few more of these and I think sex on the beach might happen."

"You had better believe it." Sam was staring at something behind me.

I turned to see Merci dressed in a flowing pink and yellow flowered mini dress. There was no question that she wore next to nothing underneath it, and I could help but remember her standing next to the bed in her electric blue high heels the last time we had danced. The yellow stiletto sandals made her long shapely legs draw even more attention than was decent, and my hands ached to touch their softness once again, which irritated me more than it should have.

"Ryan," I hadn't heard Jameron come up from behind me. "Merci is going to show me her kind of *Jazz* dancing tonight. We will look for you inside." Jameron waved before making his way over to my idea of better than sex on the beach. He took her arm and wrapped it around his, then escorted her inside the hotel with Merci clinging to his limb.

Sam let out a low whistle. "Man, oh man, how does he do it?"

I swallowed the rest of my drink down quickly and set the empty glass on the bar top louder than I had intended. "I don't know, and I'd better not hear about it in the morning."

Merci

I was ready to have fun. Two could play this game of Ryan's. His mixed messages and heated looks left me spinning. I guess tonight would either be an eye-opener or a closer for me. Either way, I intended to have fun with Jameron. He was hot, but after the incident with him in my suite earlier, I wasn't sure if he was a gentleman, didn't have time to do the job properly, or he just wasn't interested in me.

I slipped my dress on over my head, then spun around in the bathroom mirror to make sure all the necessary parts were sufficiently covered. The ladies in the shop had begged me to buy this one, and now I was glad that they had insisted. It was the perfect color of pink and yellow on me, and even though it looked baggy, it clung to my curves underneath. It dipped a little bit more than I liked down the back, but there was no crack a lackin, and that was all that mattered.

"Boy if my momma could see me now, I'd probably be send to my room to put something on." She couldn't, and she'd never hear about it from me. I curled my hair and left hanging, I pulled one side back with a yellow flower clip and wore tiny pearl earrings on each of my earlobes. I had put on all my makeup for tonight's entertainment; eye-liner and the whole deal. I dabbed on a little bit more of my perfume, before I put on, my lipstick and gloss. Just as I had finished, I heard the knock at my door, and Jameron's deep voice letting me know he would be waiting on the patio.

I must have scared him good; he was afraid to wait inside. I had to change that, or the rest of the trip would be uncomfortable for us both. I would apologize as soon as I saw him, so we would have an enjoyable evening together. I opened the door, and he turned around and started to say something, but the words never left his lips.

I twirled around in front of him just enough to let the fabric lift in the slight breeze. "Do I look okay?" After being rejected by Paul, I was still very unsure of myself; I was trying to accept that it hadn't been my fault at all.

"Oh, Merci. You do not look like the same woman I saw earlier. I will have every male on the dance floor trying to take you from me. I am honored that you asked me to go with you tonight. Thank you!"

I giggled, the way he spoke was so different from other men. He was so sincere, and he left no doubts that he meant what he said. "I wish all men were as honest as you when they spoke. Thank you for saying that. I want to apologize before we do anything else. Jameron, I am truly sorry for the way I acted earlier in my suite. It was inappropriate, and I put you in an uncomfortable position. Please forgive me; I can assure you it won't happen again."

He picked up my hand, and I watched his lips graze across my knuckles. "Merci, you are every man's dream woman. Don't ever think I was rejecting you; it just wasn't the right time for us. That doesn't mean that I didn't want you. I do, very much in fact. But you aren't ready for me. Not yet. When you are, I will be waiting. Come, I can't wait for you to show me how well you can dance."

He held my hand, so I wouldn't stumble as we strolled along the beach toward the central building of the hotel. "Tell me more about, Jamaica, Jameron. Is it similar to St. Lucia?" I loved his smooth voice when he talked; it was musical and passionate. "Do you ever plan on going back there? It must be hard to be away from your family and friends."

"Ryan is a fair boss. I can take time off to visit them whenever I want to; I can also bring them here. Most of my family now have left to live in the United States. My mother is still here, but my father died just before I left for New Orleans to follow, Lucy. I regret not being home in Jamaica with my mother during that time."

I noticed Ryan sitting at the beach bar speaking to Sam; he had a drink in his hand as usual. "Tell me more about Ryan, unless you are uncomfortable speaking about him. I'm sorry, that isn't the nicest thing to ask a handsome man when you are out on a date, is it."

He tossed back his head, and the laughter resonated throughout my bones. I couldn't help but laugh at him. "Now you understand why I didn't take you up on your previous offer. If you ever get over Mr. West, I will be waiting. I have known Ryan for many years. He has the determination and drive like no other man I have known. Soon after he married his wife Tricia, he changed. I am only telling you this, so you can understand what makes the man tick. He will do anything for someone he cares about, even when they aren't deserving of it. I will be right back."

I watched Jameron stroll over to bar; he said something to Ryan then came back to the beach for me. We both waved at Ryan who was still sitting at the bar watching us and made our way inside the hotel. Jameron led me into the restaurant and spoke for a minute with the man at the door; then we sat down at a window that overlooked the ocean. We were close to the dance floor, but far enough away where we could still hear one another talk.

"Were you talking about his wife Tricia, or Mr. Masters? Something is going on between those two; it was obvious that they were arguing about something before we ever got there. I had no idea that Troy was bringing me to Ryan's resort. But I have a good idea that he knew before he brought me here that Ryan and I had previously met. I get the feeling he's rubbing me in Ryan's face. But what can I do; he's my boss, and he pays well."

"Merci, enough talk of work. What would you like to drink?"

"Would you mind if we had a few shots first to loosen me up? After that, I want you to pick something tropical for me to drink."

"What kind of shots do you want to start with?"

I was ready for my wicked side to come out. I pursed my lips while trying to decide how nasty I wanted to get. "Fireball, and when Ryan shows up with his wife, send some over to his table as well."

Jameron's brow met in the middle, and he lowered his head before he commented. "Merci, what are you up too? Maybe you should tell me more of your story before I commit treason with you."

Ryan

I knocked on Tricia's door one more time. "Tricia, how much longer will you be?"

She was annoyed as she called out to me, "Hang on. I can't get this fucking zipper done up!"

"Then open the door and let me help you. Please, I look rather stupid standing outside in the hall knocking on my wife's door."

She pulled it open, and the looks she gave me would have killed a lesser man. "Fine, are you happy now? I broke a nail."

"Turn around. I'll pay for a manicure tomorrow. You promised me we would have dinner and go dancing, and that is what we are going to do." I had to change the way this conversation was going, or it would be a miserable night. I finished zipping up her dress, then put my hands on the front of her waist and pulled her back to me before I started nuzzling up the side of her long neck.

She giggled. "That always tickles; stop, or I will pee my pants."

I slapped her on the behind as she pulled away from me and walked back over to the bed to pick up her purse. "You look beautiful, Tricia. I can't wait to show you off on the dance floor." I hadn't really paid attention to what she was wearing before I spoke. She did look lovely, but she wasn't wearing what I would consider a dancing dress.

"Are you going to be able to move in that dress? I am planning on dancing with you most of the night."

"I am pregnant you know, and I hadn't planned on being on my feet all night long."

I smiled and moved closer to her; then I cupped her cheek to keep her wandering eyes focused on me. "Does that mean you would like to retire earlier? I would like to spend the night making love to my wife." I leaned in and kissed her quickly on the mouth.

"We will see. I would like that too, Ry. I'm still going through that morning sickness crap, but we will see what happens. Okay? Oh, uh who else is going to be at our table?"

"It will just be the two of us. I want to bring back what we used to have, but I can't if you keep pushing me away. I hoped we could spend the night together, even if you aren't feeling up to making love, I would like to sleep with you in my arms. Come, I can hear the music from up here. What would you like to eat for dinner?"

"Why don't you choose for me."

We made our way inside the restaurant; I had made earlier arrangements with Badrick to have a table ready for us by the window that overlooked the beach. Zamora greeted us at the door. "Mr. and Mrs. West, your table is ready. Please follow me."

I moved Tricia in front of me, and we stayed close behind Zamora as we wound our way through the restaurant. The jazz band was playing a sultrier song; the couples were already grinding and gyrating to the sensations the music provoked.

We reached our table, and I thanked Zamora. "Tricia, let me get your seat." I moved once again behind her and pulled her chair out from under the table, so she could sit down. Then I hurried over to the other side to avoid having another couple run into me. "Wow, this group is fantastic. I'm glad we were able to get them booked in here for the next few months; they will be here for the holidays." We both picked up our menu, and I read the appetizer choices out loud. "Does anyone of those sound like something you might want to try, Tricia?"

She glanced up at me and was just about to speak when movement on the dance floor caught her attention. "Ryan, is that Jameron? OMG, who is he with? It sure looks like he'll be getting some tonight."

I couldn't help but notice the two of them on the dance floor together, especially since Tricia was still enthralled with their movements. Miss, *better than sex on the beach* had become *orgasmic on the dance floor* for anyone who wanted to watch, which

I did, but shouldn't have. I picked up my glass of water and swallowed quickly to wash the covetous lump of desire down my throat.

"Jesus Christ!" I spoke the words louder than I had intended to and felt Tricia kick my ankle from under the table.

"You ought to say something to Jameron about his behavior. Do you think an employee should act like that where his peers can see him?"

"He is off the clock, but I will say something to him about it tomorrow. I guarantee he won't like what I have to say, either."

Tricia continued to study the menu, and I tried to focus on mine, but the girl who had been on my mind ever since she arrived on this island was so close I could have touched her. The contrast of Jam's dark hands sliding up and down on Merci's silky white thighs left me seeing red.

Our server stepped in between the table and my view of the passionate couple who looked as if they were having the sex on the dance floor, and just in time. "Good evening, what can I get you both to drink?"

"Bring me a tall Bourbon, straight. Tricia, what would you like to drink?"

Merci

"Thank you, Jameron. Are you sure you can't come inside? I don know bout you, but I don want to sleep yet. Please! Wait, you have to cause I'm afraid of snakes. Jameron, I'm pletely serious. What if I swear you won't do anything. I swear it on my right hand. See?" I stuck my arm up straight into the air.

"I, insert your name here, swear we won't have sex unless you tell me you aren't afraid of snakes, insert your name here. There, now do you believe me?" I grabbed onto his forearm, so the porch would stop rocking. Then I and kicked one shoe off first into the air, and then the other onto the beach.

Jameron's full lips lifted on both sides "Merci, I will stay with you, but I will sleep on top of the covers. Here, lean on your door while I get your shoe off the beach before somebody trips on it."

"There's nobody on the beach but the snakes. Hurry, Jameron before they bite your toes." I waited for him to bend over then said, "You do have a nice butt, Jameron. Come on, hold my hand so you don fall and we'll go inside my sweet suite. Can I at least kiss you good night on the porch? It's our first date, and we can kiss good night."

Jameron set my shoes down together by the door, then he took both my hands in each one of his and lifted them above my head pressing them into the door above me. He pushed me back against the door; almost every inch of his hard body was touching mine. "Then I will make this good night kiss count. Merci, I had a most enjoyable night with you. Thank you for the perfect first date, mon cheri."

I couldn't see his eyes as his face neared mine, so I closed my eyes and waited, mouth open and breathless for his kiss. He slanted his mouth over mine, and his tongue danced and swirled slowly around and around. He continued to kiss me, his deep assault on my senses started a different kind of heat building inside of me.

"Don't stop, please don't stop, Jameron."

Chapter Twelve

Ryan

The evening had been almost unbearable for me to sit through. As soon as Merci noticed Tricia and I sitting at the table near to the one she and Jameron were at, her and Jam's movements together seemed to become even more seductive and provocative. She sent a round of Fireball whiskey shots to our table, and I quickly downed them both; I needed to feel the fire burning down my throat and scorching my empty soul.

Tricia had only wanted to dance once with me, and it had been chaste; as if we were children dancing for the first time in front of grownups afraid to touch one another lest we get caught. The night had been a disaster, and I wanted nothing more than the girl who had teased me all night long on the dance floor with my employee.

"Are you ready to go back to your room, sweetheart?"

"Yes, I'm sorry, this pregnancy is kicking my butt. I don't want to have any more kids after this one; I hope that's okay with you."

"I would like a couple more, but let's just see what happens after this one, okay. Have you thought about what I asked you earlier? Can I spend the night with you?"

We were on her floor walking toward her suite. "I don't feel like having sex, but if you want to sleep next to me on the bed, that would be all right. I'm sorry, Ry. You understand, don't you?"

I took the key card from her hand and opened the door to her suite, then waved her inside in front of me. "No, I don't, actually.

Tricia, I have needs. I've been doing a lot of reading on women and pregnancies. I read that most women are hornier when they are pregnant because they don't have to worry about getting that way since they already are. Don't I do it for you anymore?"

I shut the door behind me and stepped closer to her. "Tricia, I love you, and I've told you before how much I want to watch our baby growing inside you." I put my hand on her belly and met her eyes. "Will you shower with me? I'd love to cover your body with soap and feel the baby between us. I want to feel the heaviness of your breasts as they begin to fill with mother's milk. I want to suck on them. The picture of our child latching on as you feed him or her in my mind fills me with so much joy. Please, Tricia, let's shower together."

"I hate to disappoint you, but there is no way in hell that I'm going to breastfeed. Do you know what that does to a women's tits? It's not going to happen. Besides, you've got to help me take care of the baby too and you can't if I'm doing all the work. Sorry, Ry. It's not happening."

"So are you referring to the shower, or nursing our child?"

"I'm afraid both tonight; I'm tired. Did you also read that pregnant woman need more sleep than usual, and they don't always want to have sex because it gets uncomfortable? Ryan, I don't want to argue with you anymore tonight. Maybe you should just go back to your own room to sleep."

I shook my head back and forth slowly. "I can't believe you are doing this again. You know what, Tricia. When you decide you want to resume relations with me, then let me know. For now, I'll keep to myself, and you can do the same. Have a great night. I'll feel much better after I go back to my room and jack off!"

I hurried out of her room and slammed the door on the way out to make sure she knew I meant business. What a fool I was. She would never change, and I would be stuck in this loveless, lonely relationship for the rest of my life. I wasn't leaving my child with that woman, and I knew she'd fight me tooth and nail for every last dime if I tried. At least I knew exactly where I stood with her now and I didn't have to pretend anymore.

I left the hotel and took off down the beach determined to stay out of Tricia's hair the rest of the time we were here. She had infuriated me, and she had left me with no one to turn to in my need to forget about the girl who had taunted me all night long on the dance floor.

As I neared Merci's suite, I saw them both pressed up against her door in a passionate kiss, and in my state of mind, things were now even worse than had been before. "Jesus Christ, Jameron. Fuck her inside, not out here on the front porch."

Merci

Our first kiss continued longer than I had expected, and the sexy man who had pressed every hard inch of his body against me was obviously as turned on as I was, but he was right. I wasn't ready for more from him yet. I was prepared to break off the kiss when I heard Ryan's tormented voice say something nasty to us as he hurried past.

Jameron stepped away from me. "I apologize for what Ryan just said, Merci. I will speak to him tomorrow and let him know we were only kissing and that it was all my fault. I will ask him to apologize to you as well."

I chewed on my lips while listening to Jameron speak. "Don worry bout it, Jameron. We were just kissing, and if he wants to b'lieve something else happened, then let him. Will you still sleep in my bed with me? I won bother you for more than that; I just can't fall asleep without seeing that snake coming toward me in the shower."

"Give me your key, Merci. I will stay with you until you are sound asleep." Jameron opened the front door and went in the direction of the small kitchen. "I am going to get us both some ice water from the kitchen while you get yourself ready for bed."

I still was using the guest bedroom and bathroom; the other one had too many vivid memories. I was glad that I'd brought regular pajamas with me to sleep in, and put on a pair of those before I brushed my teeth.

When I came out of the bathroom, Jameron was sitting on the chair in the corner. "Merci, once you are asleep, I must go to the hotel to sleep. Ryan is expecting some investors in the morning, and I must be there to make sure their rooms are ready. Will you be okay here alone once I go?"

I had been just fine with him sleeping on the bed next to me, but I didn't have the right to keep him from his duties. "Of course, Jameron. Just wait until I fall asleep and you can go any time after that. I really had a fun night. Are you still taking me dancing on the weekend?"

"Merci, I can't wait to show you my favorite place in town. Yes, we will dance the night away so prepare yourself. Now climb under the covers before I change my mind and stay. No woman has the right to look so beautiful in flannel pajamas."

I giggled. "You are good for my ego, Jameron." I took the glass of ice water from his outstretched hand and guzzled some of it down.

"Thank you, I needed that." I handed the glass back to him, then stood up on my tiptoes and kissed his cheek.

"Good night, Jam, I will see you in the morning."

"That reminds me, you are on your own until afternoon. Troy and Ryan will be showing his guests around his property in the morning. I will let you know if anything changes. Now get under the covers girl and go to sleep."

I did as I was told, and Jameron climbed on top of the covers and lay down on the pillow next to me. I let out the most unladylike yawn, and he smiled. "Good night."

Ryan

My head was pounding. Not only had I had too much to drink, but the fight between Tricia and me had brought on a different kind of a headache, and after seeing the couple next door locked in an embrace had gotten much worse.

I climbed out of my bed and decided to see if a shower would help ease the pain. I turned the water to the hottest setting then as soon as it was warm enough I stepped under the spray. I adjusted the shower settings to pulse and stood there letting the water do its magic.

I had important guests coming in the morning, and I had to be at the top of my game. If I didn't get rid of this headache soon, I'd never be able to sleep.

After standing there for about twenty minutes, I felt the tension start to leave my shoulders. I shut off the water, and went back into the bathroom to grab a few more ibuprofens, then went into the kitchen for a bottle of water.

I walked outside onto my patio and sat down to breath in the fresh ocean air. That's when I heard a woman whimpering, and listened more intently. *Was that Merci?* She continued to cry; then I heard her yell out, *'Help me!'*

I jumped up from my chair; I knew Jameron had gone inside her suite. "I'll kill that son of a bitch!" I grabbed the master key from off the top of my dresser and stormed out my door and ran down the beach.

I opened the door and ran into Merci's suite. "Where are you, Merci?"

I heard her cry out again from the guest bedroom. *'Get away from me!'* I tore through the dark entrance and threw open the door to the guestroom. Merci was alone on the bed with the sheets twisted around her lower legs. Jameron was nowhere to be seen, and she was still asleep.

The snake, she must be dreaming about the snake. I rushed to the end of the bed and carefully pulled her legs free of the sheets. That seemed to calm her down a little, but she still whimpered. I climbed up onto the bed to comfort her.

I slid my arm underneath her body, the pajamas she had on were damp and sweaty from her struggles. "Merci, I'm here now, you are safe darlin'. I smoothed the damp locks off her face. "You are so warm, Merci. Wake up; it's me, Ryan. We need to get you cooled off."

Merci woke and sat straight up in bed. "Help me; I can't move!"

"That's because you've got yourself all wrapped up in your pajamas. Merci, let me help you get untangled." I sat up next to her; she was still groggy and not fully awake, but apparently terrified. I grabbed onto the bottom of her pajama top and lifted it over her head, then laid her back down on the bed next to me before removing her bottoms.

Her thrashing slowed to a stop, but she was covered in sweat. I started blowing across her damp skin to cool her down. Then I heard her ask, "Ryan, how did you get in here, and what are you doing?"

What was I doing? I hadn't put anything on after I showered, and I was lying in her bed with my pursed lips inches from her flesh. I got up on my elbow to look at her. The glow of the moon just outside the bedroom window illuminated both our bodies. We were glistening under its heavenly light.

"I heard you calling out for help from my room and thought you were in trouble. Why didn't you tell me you were having nightmares about the snake? I could have been here with you at night to make sure you weren't afraid to sleep. Merci, I still care about you; I always will."

"I care about you too, but this can't happen. Ryan, you've got a child on the way. You shouldn't be here."

I slowly circled my finger around her navel, then ran it straight up her damp skin between her heaving breasts. I stopped on the pulse beating at the base of her neck. "I want you, Merci. From the way your heart is beating, you want me just as much."

"But…"

I removed my finger from her neck and placed it over her full mouth. "No buts, tonight. Please, Merci. Let me make love to you one more time before I can't anymore."

I stared into her eyes as I outlined her lips with my finger. "Darlin, I know what buttons to push to make you scream. Not because you are afraid, but because I make you feel something. Let me show you what I mean."

I continued watching her face as I ran my finger back over the pulse on her neck and lower to swirl over one of her hard nipples, just grazing over it light enough to make it push out even harder. Then I slowly did the same to the other one as I focused on her eyes. "I can tell how good this feels, Merci. Do you know your eyes change color when you are in the throes of passion? The color deepens, and your breath hitches in your throat."

I smiled before I leaned my head closer and kissed the side of her mouth. My face was inches from hers, and I felt her hot breath on the side of my neck. I pressed my mouth over hers, then slowly ran my tongue down over her slick skin. I laved around each one of her breasts then covered each of her nipples and pulled them into my mouth as I gently bit down until she cried out.

Merci

Watching Ryan do the things to me that he did so well was almost unbearable. He elicited such pleasure in some ways, yet when he bit down on my nipples, it was almost painful, but I didn't want him to stop. "Oh my God, Ryan. Please…I…Oh, don't stop!"

"You like that don't you, Darlin'? I like it too; your skin is like melted butter under my fingers. Salty and all slick. I know somewhere else that's slick as well, shall I continue?"

I had no control over my body when he lowered his hand. I started to buck and squirm when his fingers found the place I wanted them most. He pinched and squeezed my clit, then slowly slid one finger in and out of my opening.

"You are so wet, Merci. You like that don't you? Do you want more, Darlin?"

"You know I do, Ryan." I stumbled over his name as the first wave hit me. He put more than one finger inside me now as he pumped them in and out then stopped them deep inside me as I pulsed around his digits.

"Say my name, Merci. I want to hear you call out my name." He continued to pump his fingers into me.

"Ryan, oh my god, don't st…stop!" Another wave of pleasure started.

"You are so beautiful, Merci. So fucking beautiful." Suddenly he had his face between my legs, and his tongue continued where his fingers left off. I don't know how many times I climaxed like that; I only knew that each time I did, he was there to make sure that each one of them was more intense and pleasurable than the time before.

My voice was unrecognizable when I whispered his name. "Ryan, please. I need to feel you inside me. Please!"

"I'm sorry, Merci. I just can't do that." He sat up on his knees; his arousal was very evident. He put his fingers into his mouth and sucked on them before pulling them out. "You taste so sweat."

Then he got off the bed and walked out of the bedroom. I heard the front door close, then felt the hot wet tears as they rolled down my cheeks and onto my neck.

Ryan

I walked back to my room regretting what I had done. It had taken all my willpower to leave her lying on the bed. I had already done more than I should have with Merci. The problem was that I was still a married man with a baby on the way, and my marriage would never last if I had stayed and spent the night making love to Merci. There was no doubt that I loved her.

I entered my suite and went back into the outdoor shower. I had a raging hard-on, and there was only one thing I could do for that now. I turned the hot water on and pumped my member until it was dry and limp. Then I dried off and slid under the covers of my empty king bed, and tried to sleep.

I tossed and turned for what seemed like hours. When I finally slept, it was haunted by the vision of Merci's cries, and the hurt look in her eyes when I left her alone in her bed.

Chapter Thirteen

Ryan

The alarm had been blaring; I didn't know for how long before I finally shut it off. The clock said eight fifteen, and I was meeting my guests at nine this morning for breakfast. I climbed out of my bed and hurried into the shower. I turned the water temperature as cold as I could stand it to help me clear my head and wake up.

I finished dressing, then called Jameron on the house phone that was standard in each room. "Yes, Pheora, could you page, Jameron Sebastian? Thank you. I will wait." I had an apology to make. He hadn't spent the night with Merci, and if he had, I wouldn't be filled with remorse for my actions. He was a good friend, and I couldn't lose him because of my stupidity.

I heard his rich voice answer. "Hey, Jam. It's your asshole for a boss, Ryan. Listen, I need to apologize for the things I said to you and Merci both last night. I'm sorry, neither one of you deserved that. I understand, Yes, I will apologize to her when I see her. You are right again my friend."

I listened as he went on to tell me how hard it was for Merci to get to sleep at night after the snake incident in her shower. "Yes, I understand. It was very thoughtful of you to be there for her. Have our guests arrived yet? Good, I'm on my way. Listen, would you please have a black coffee ready for me when I get there. I overslept. If they arrive before I do, get them a table with an ocean view. Have you seen, Troy yet this morning? Tell him I am on my way."

I hurried out of my suite glancing toward Merci's rooms as I walked by. I had to apologize for my behavior as soon as I saw her. I decided to make every effort to make sure we were never alone together while she was here. If my marriage was going to last, I had to pretend that Miss Lachance didn't exist.

I saw Troy getting off the elevator just as I entered the hotel. "Hey buddy, how was your evening? You missed some great entertainment last night. Where did you go?"

"Last time I was here I found a little business in town that interested me. I'm trying to buy it."

"Really, that surprises me. Do you plan on spending more time in St. Lucia then?"

"Why not, I'd like to come over here a couple of times a year; if I had a small business that I could work on then what would stop me? I stopped and said hi to Patricia. I thought you were going to be there last night. What happened, lovers quarrel?"

"We can't talk about this right now, but it is none of your business. It looks like our guests have arrived."

Troy and I walked into the restaurant together and made our way to the table where George Tanner and Douglas Brandt sat with Jameron waiting for us. Thankfully Jameron had a decanter of coffee and cups waiting for us.

They stood up as we approached and we all shook hands. Then we sat down, and I poured the coffee. "Our server will be here with our menus, gentlemen. I suggest the New York steak and eggs with biscuits and gravy."

Merci

I was so sore when I woke up. It felt as if I'd spent the night wrestling. I had, with my conscience and my feelings for Ryan. His rejection of me had hurt even harder this time. Why hadn't I learned the last time this had happened? I couldn't keep doing this to myself anymore.

Paul's rejection of me had been understandable once he told me he was gay, but Ryan kept sending me mixed signals. First, we were on; then we were off. Were we on or off this time? I knew the answer to that had to remain off. Like he had told me more than once. He was going to be a father, and he needed to make his unhappy marriage work. So why had he shown up and done everything to me except the final act of intercourse with me? Wasn't what we had done together last night cheating? It wasn't okay for a man who was supposed to be happily ever after married to make love to me as he had with his fingers and his mouth and not call that cheating, was it?

I had to forget about him; let him go and move on with my life. But first I needed to talk to my girls; their sweet voices always cheered me up. I gave the hotel operate my credit card information and waited for her to connect my call.

My mother answered the phone. "Mom, I sure have missed you guys. No, I'm okay, just homesick for my two babies. Yes, I'm sure that's all it is. How are you doing with them? They are good girls, aren't they?" We continued to chat for a few more minutes; I was sure my mom was checking up on me, I had been emotional when she had first answered. One day I would tell her about Ryan and the first time I met him, but not now. I needed to have that discussion with her face to face.

She handed the phone to Maddie first. "Hello, Maddie. Grandma tells me you have been such a big helper. I am going to town this weekend, and I know two little girls who need a special surprise from this island. Yes, it is surrounded by water, and no I am not afraid. I'm going to have fun at the beach today. Which one should I wear? Okay, I love you too, now let me speak to Allie."

I spent a few more minutes on the phone; it had been a good idea to call them. Hearing my family's voices made me feel better and even more determined to keep my distance from the man who kept on breaking my heart.

I ordered room service, and while I waited for it to get here, I took a quick shower before I put on the blue bikini that Maddie had told me to wear. It had a fun blue and white striped cover up to wear over the top, and I also had matching blue flip-flops.

I was dressed and had just finished putting my hair into a big bun on the back of my head when I heard the knock on the front door. "Room Service."

Ryan

We had taken our time and had discussed trivial things during breakfast. We had all had our fill of coffee, and I signaled to Badrick that it was time for the cocktail refreshments.

"I'm glad you enjoyed breakfast. Badrick is bringing us a few pitchers of our new beach cocktails. They will be featured at our all of our bars on the property. Gentleman, enjoy some of our new drink concoctions." Badrick and Sam both brought in a tray with our newest drinks in a glass and a pitcher full of each kind and set them on the table in front of us.

The first drink was served in a wide mouth jar with old bay chunky salt coating the rim. There was a crispy piece of skewered peppered bacon sticking into a celery stock. "This is our Bloody Bacon in the Sun, Mary. Make sure you dunk your bacon into the juice after you try the drink. This is the perfect way to start your mornings on the beach."

"When you are ready, I would like to make a toast. Gentlemen, Raise your glass. "Out with the old, in with the new. Cheers to our future and all that we do."

The 'Bloody Mary' was a hit. I couldn't wait to see their reaction to the next one. "This one is called Better than sex on the beach. I hope it brings you some if that's what you desire."

We all laughed at my statement, then I watched all of them taste Sam's masterpiece. "What do you think? I know it's a little sweet first thing in the morning but wait just a minute. It packs a powerful punch." And so did the girl who stopped just outside of the window we all sat next to.

Troy and Jameron both started choking on their cocktails, and I heard the older of my guests, George, mumble something under his breath about making a fortune if you could bottle what that girl had to offer.

I, on the other hand, wanted to run outside and cover Merci with a large blanket so that no one could see her perfection. More than one unattached male in the restaurant made their way over to the picture window and watched as she covered herself with lotion. I heard more than one person clear their throat when she bent over in front of the glass.

"Jameron, could I have a word with you in the lobby?"

"Yes, Mr. West, what can I do for you?"

I looked behind me to see if they were all still enthralled with the girl in the cabana. "I really don't need Merci's services this afternoon, and seeing the effect she has on guests, I'm not sure that she would do much but distract them. Would you mind letting her know that her services aren't needed and that I will speak to her tomorrow?"

Jameron nodded his head slightly as he raised his eyebrows. "I will let her know, but you still owe her an apology. I will return, don't start the next round of drinks without me."

I laughed out loud. "If we can keep serving the men in front of the window, they will be putty in my hands before noon. Hurry back."

Merci

I grabbed my beach bag, a bottle of water, sunscreen and my headphones. I had seen some unusual looking sun cabanas on the beach the other day, and since I had no intentions of sun burning again, I decided to search for one of them to spend my morning at.

It was still quite early, and the beaches weren't crowded at all yet. I found one nearer to the hotel and set my things down on the bench before I began covering myself with lotion.

I bent over and smoothed the cream over the back of my legs first. Then I reached everywhere that I could on my back before I covered my arms with the lotion. Next, I rubbed the thick liquid into the front of my thighs, then squirted more onto my stomach and belly. I slathered the cream all over the tops of my breasts then put the lid back on the tube of sunblock.

I'd put a higher SPF on my face just before I left my rooms, so after I put on my sunglasses, I spread the beach towel over the raised platform and took my time climbing on top of to make sure that my bath sheet stayed in place. I plugged my music into my ears and got ready to stay put.

"Good morning, Merci. How are you doing today? Did you sleep well after I left?"

I was just starting to relax to my music when I heard Jameron's voice. "Eventually I slept. I am enjoying the sun this morning. How are you doing? Did Ryan's guests show up?"

Jameron cleared his throat before he spoke. "Yes, they did. He wanted to let you know that he won't need you at all today. They are going to be busy all morning long and possibly the rest of the afternoon as well. He asked me to tell you to enjoy your day off, and he will see you tomorrow."

"Thank you, Jam. Maybe I'll explore the beach after I'm finished here. Wait, will you also be busy all day?"

His smile was so engaging. "I am never too busy for you, Merci. Call me if you need me."

"Jam, actually…before you go could you undo my swimsuit top, so I don't get a weird line?"

"Wh…what did you say?"

I need you to undo my swimsuit top, so I don't get any strange tan lines, please, it's so difficult for me to move where I'm at."

"Of course, Merci. But first, you must promise me not to sit up unless you are fully dressed. It is a family beach after all, and too many young innocent boys might be distracted by your lack of clothing and your loveliness."

I couldn't help but giggle. "That is too hilarious; young boys shouldn't be out here looking at old ladies like me." I laid down flat. "I'm ready when you are." His warm hand grazed my back which made me shiver.

Why did it always feel so good to undo a bra strap, or in this case a bikini top. I sighed, "Jameron, that, correction you gave me goosebumps. Not to worry, I don't plan on leaving this spot for a while."

"Very good. I will be inside the restaurant if you need any more of my help."

Ryan

Jameron hurried back into the restaurant and avoided my eyes. I leaned in a spoke to him, so the others didn't hear me. "What in the hell was that all about? How do I explain that to my colleagues? We aim to please, and we undress fair maidens in distress, or rather undress them on the beach. Keep your hands to yourself, Jam."

He glared back at me and whispered through gritted teeth, "And what do I tell the girl, I can't help you because there is a group of lonely old men watching you from the window. Ryan, if you want the girl for yourself, then you had better stop leading your wife on. Do the right thing, for everyone's sake."

He sat down next to Troy at the table, and Troy laughed out loud. "Good show, Jameron. I didn't think you had it in you. Gentlemen, should we take this party somewhere else, I do believe that girl has you all tongue-tied. Ryan, should we take this upstairs to your office?"

For Merci's sake and my sanity, I decided that was the safest idea. "Gentlemen, I hate to spoil your fun, but we've got a lot to talk about. Shall we take this upstairs?

They begrudgingly stood up and backed up from the table, making sure she remained in their sights for as long as was possible. "We'll follow you, Troy." I leaned over to Jameron and whispered. "You'd think they'd never seen a female before, Jesus Christ. Maybe we should take them out to *a titty* bar later on."

Jam surprised me with his answer. "Is the kettle calling the pot black? If I remember correctly your face was glued to the window with the others."

"Now wait just a minute, are you jealous, Jam? Is that what this is all about? Merci is fair game, just don't hurt her." We were far behind the other three, which was a good thing considering the argument we were having.

Jameron stopped in the middle of the hall and waited for the others to enter the elevator. As soon as the doors closed he faced me. "Once again the kettle and the pot comes to mind. Ryan, from what I have seen, you have done more to hurt that girl since she has been here than I've ever seen you treat another person. If you care for her, which I believe you do, then you had better do something to fix this. Merci is a caring, beautiful young woman who doesn't deserve what you are doing. I'm very attracted to the girl as well, but I've held back knowing she loves you. Yes you, you pig-headed stubborn man. The girl is head over heels crazy for you, and you can't make up your mind which woman you want. You can't have them both, Ryan."

We stood there, nose to nose. I should be mad at him for what he had said to me. I was his boss, but he was just telling the truth. "Jam, I admire your courage. You aren't too bright though. I could fire you for talking to me that way."

"Then fire me, and when you do, I will say more things that you should hear. Ryan, we are friends, we have been since my brother passed. Now you are like a brother to me, and I want you to be happy. But, I won't let something that amazing slip through my fingers because you can't make up your mind."

I put my hand on the back of his neck and pulled him in close to me. "Thanks, I needed to hear that, and you are absofuckinglutely correct. I do need to make a decision and stick to it. We'd better get upstairs before Troy has the whole business sold out from under our noses. After you, Jam." We walked next to each other then stopped to wait for the elevator.

"Ryan, that reminds me. Why do I get the feeling Mr. Troy Masters isn't as good a friend as I once thought he was of yours?"

Merci

I carefully turned over once again then did up my swimsuit top. I was finished baking in the sun; the ocean was calling my name, and the beach was busier than it had been when I had first stepped foot on it this morning.

I gathered my things and put them in the bag I had, then slipped on my matching cover, and picked up my sandals. I wanted to feel the sand between my toes as I walked. The only thing I didn't have was a hat to shade my face. Oh well, you only live once.

I stepped into the salty ocean; it was cold on my sunbaked skin, but I soon adjusted to the temperature and stood in the water watching the ebb and flow of the tide swirl around my feet and calves repeatedly.

I had listened to the music earlier to try and stop thoughts from driving me crazy. There was nothing to stop them now, and just like the ocean, each thought, sentence, and feeling since meeting Ryan hit me over and over again. What was I doing here? Was this a working vacation, or was it Troy's way of getting back at Ryan for something that happened between them sometime in their past. I had started paying closer attention to the interaction Troy and Ryan had with one another when they were in a room together. There was definitely bad blood between the two of them.

So why had Troy brought me, of all people to this island? What was the real reason I was here? I decided that I needed to ask Troy for the answers myself. Being here and seeing Ryan in this paradise wasn't worth losing my sanity for. Remembering how easy it was for Ryan to have me begging for him like I had done last night and the reality of our relationship or rather the lack of one hurt deeply.

My decision was made, I'd confront Troy later this evening, and if his answer didn't satisfy me, then I would ask him to send me back home.

Chapter Fourteen

Ryan

We were only a few floors above the beach, but my seat at the head of this table had been placed here purposely so I could see the ocean as I worked. Now my eyes couldn't help but watch the girl standing alone in the sea.

"Ryan, did you have anything to add, or have you already forgotten what we are here for?" Troy's sneer when he spoke made me uncomfortable. He was up to something, and I still hadn't figured out what it was.

"Not at all, watching that girl helped me make a decision. Gentlemen, there is an exclusive club in town that caters to more of the elite customers who visit this island. The girls are beautiful who work there. Would anyone in this room protest a visit there this evening?" They all shook their heads no.

"Good, then it is settled. Jameron, could you call, Jasmine and make the arrangements for four of us? I will need you to be there with us of course. I'll ask Bartholomew to watch the resort this evening.

"Of course. Did you want the reservations for dinner or the later show?"

"Shall we make it dinner at six?" George and Douglas both nodded in agreement. "Troy, what would you like to do?"

"I'll let you know. I must check my schedule first then I'll get back with you. Jam, go ahead and make the reservations for four, and if anything changes I will call and cancel myself."

"Very good. Gentlemen, please feel free to visit the rest of the property, I'll leave both your names at the bar; unlimited cocktails and food are yours for the asking. We will meet back down in the front lobby by the elevators at six this evening."

I waited for the others to leave the room. "Troy, do you have a minute?" I wanted to get to the bottom of this animosity between us.

"Sure, but make it quick, I'm meeting someone soon."

I waited for Jameron to leave with the others, then poured myself another drink from the decanter that still had Seaside Sangria inside. "Have a seat."

Troy stood by the door waiting to leave, he ran his hand through his thick light brown hair, then sat down. "It's your dime. What's up?"

"Why don't you enlighten me? What is going on with you? Why is there so much antagonism toward me lately? What have I done to make you so resentful, and what is going on between you and my wife, Patricia?"

Troy laughed out loud before he looked at me. "You can't honestly sit there and tell me you don't know? Come on, Ryan. You can't be that naive or that stupid.

"You are wrong. I don't know what you are talking about. If I did, we wouldn't be sitting here. Tell me. Maybe I should have Patricia join us in here. Does this concern her?" He wouldn't look at me now.

"It does, wow. How long have you been sleeping with my wife? Is the baby yours?"

Then he turned an incredulous face toward me. "Baby? What are you talking about, is Patricia pregnant?"

"You didn't know?" From the look on his face, I could tell this was a surprise to him. "You've spent so much time with her lately; I'm surprised she didn't say anything to you before."

"Congrats, when is the happy event?" He didn't sound too thrilled when he asked.

"I...we don't have a date yet. I just found out a month ago myself." I glanced down at my watch. "We'll talk about this later; I've got to work on a few things before we meet up tonight."

"Sure, me too."

Merci

Maybe this afternoon would be an excellent time to visit the spa. I wanted another hair removal treatment, and my feet and hands needed attention after spending so much time on the beach. I made my way to the hotel and wandered the halls until I reached the day salon and spa.

"Hello, miss. What can we help you with?" The receptionist was young and so pretty; her skin was the color of rich honey with eyes to match.

"Lakyta, what a pretty name for such a pretty girl. What does it mean?"

"Found treasure. My parents were told once they couldn't have any children and adopted me. Thank you for your kind words, miss. What did you need done?"

"Do you have any package deals? I need a whole lot of work."

She giggled, then shook her head. "I wish all our patrons looked like you. Here is the paper with our monthly specials listed at the bottom. This month we are running a buy one package get the second one, half price. Our busiest day is always Friday, so today we have many openings for the different services still available."

"Can I take this to read, I need a few minutes to decide how much money I have to spend."

She smiled, then turned away. I was already forgotten. I sat down in the comfortable oversized chair and began reading through the specials.

"Mrs. West, it is so nice to see you here again. I missed you the other day when you came in for your massage. Trixie tells me you are expecting. When is the baby due?"

I peeked over the paper, Tricia hadn't yet figured out who I was, and the less she saw of me, the better. I listened in on their conversation. I hadn't wanted to ask Ryan anything about the baby, so my luck at hearing the information right from her would appease my curiosity.

"I'm almost through the first trimester. The baby is due in six months. You can see why I am so desperate for a massage. Soon I won't be able to lay on my stomach. Is, Wisteria, available, she has the best hands."

"Let me check. Oh, you are in luck, she just is finishing up with her last appointment. Would you like me to show you back to room four, you can get undressed, and I will let her know you are waiting. Follow me."

"Hmm, according to my calculations, Tricia was already expecting the first night Ryan spent with me. I might have to ask him about that." I was trying to remember everything he had told me that night about her.

"Miss, have you decided on a service?"

"You know what, I've got a date out on the town sight-seeing and dancing on Saturday, I will do the deluxe package. Can I start in the sauna first?"

I undressed, then wrapped myself in the luxurious towel. I walked into the sauna and hurried over to the corner, so I could be alone and think. The first night I'd spent with Ryan was etched clearly in my memory. Why wouldn't be, it was the beginning of my new life and the end of feeling like I was a nobody. I went over the conversation in my mind from the beginning of the night, or at least what I could remember of that part. I'd had too much to drink, and some of it was a blur.

We then went to the hotel, correction, his hotel. Now I remembered him getting angry when I mentioned his name. He didn't want me to know who he was. I probably wouldn't have either. The name, Ryan West, wasn't a household name, but I had perhaps read it in the paper some time in my life.

I remembered our conversation that night, and the one just before he ripped my skirt off. That would always make me smile. He was determined to get that ratty thing off. I remembered the rest of the night clearly after that. His varied talents as far as pleasing women were concerned left nothing to be desired, except for him inside of me at the end of the night.

"Now you are getting greedy, Merci." I hadn't noticed the other woman enter the sauna.

"Excuse me?"

"Sorry, just going over my lines for the school play. Do you have the current time?"

"I've been in here for a few minutes, and it was three when I first entered the salon."

"Thanks, on to my next quest. Enjoy the steam, that corner is the best for opening up your pores and your mind. I'd move over there if I were you."

Ryan

I'd had enough to drink already, and the day was young. I wasn't meeting the others for a few more hours. *Oh, well*. I might as well enjoy my time on the island holding a full glass in my hand since everything else had gone to shit. The girls in the gentlemen's club were exotic looking, and a night of adult entertainment might be just what I needed, except there would be no one waiting for me when I got back to my room.

I was on my way to the beach bar to discuss the new drinks with Sam. The men had enjoyed all the ones he'd provided for us earlier. I wanted to thank him for being so creative. The smoked bacon added to the Mary's was an excellent choice, and he needed to know how appreciative they others were of that one. His inventiveness would be a big payoff for the hotel.

I started down the hallway and heard arguing near the elevator which was just around the corner. I stopped in my shoes to listen as soon as I recognized my wife's voice.

"What does it matter to you anyway. We are done, you made sure of that in New York a few months ago when you showed up with that little twit on your arm. You knew I would be waiting for you. Let go of my arm; you are hurting me."

I almost stepped around the corner to see who she was speaking to but stopped when I heard Troy's irritated answer. "We spent almost every weekend before that night together. Patricia, I just want to know if the child is mine. You are not taking it away from me. I won't let Ryan take something else of mine from me."

I couldn't breathe as I listened to Troy and Tricia quarreling. Then the words that were being said by each of them began to register. I needed to hear her answer, everything I was doing depended on her response to Troy's question.

They must have gotten on the elevator together. I punched the wall next to me. "Christ, my timing has been off for way too long." The conversation they had played over and over in my mind.

I had to finish that talk with Troy. Every time I had tried, he'd laughed it off, or made an excuse to leave the room. Tonight, I would make sure he was good and drunk; then I'd confront him. If I didn't get the answers I needed from him I would question Tricia.

"They were sleeping together for months. Months! I'll be damned if that child is mine." There was nothing I could do until later. For now, I decided to be as calm as I could and act as if nothing had changed. But it had, my entire marriage had been a lie, my one chance at happiness was somewhere on this island running around in a skimpy blue bikini, and I couldn't let her get away from me without finding out the truth.

I stopped by the bar and thanked Sam for the best drinks on the planet, then hurried down the beach to see if I could find Merci. I needed to see her, but more than anything I needed to apologize for the way I had treated her. She had been the only one who had been honest with me. According to Jam, he told her he wouldn't pursue her until he was sure that her and I were finished. He did say to me she wasn't done with me; his exact words were 'She is crazy head over heels for you.'

That made me smile. Jameron was an excellent judge of character, and if he felt that coming from her, then it must be true. He was right, if there was a chance of happiness with that woman, I couldn't let it slip through my fingers. I had to fight for what I wanted, and tonight, I'd come to blows with Troy Masters to get the information I sought. I was finished playing these games with him, and my whore of a wife.

I arrived at Merci's suite and knocked at the door. I listened but didn't hear anything from inside. She could be napping, or she could be sitting out on the enclosed patio. I walked around to the front and peeked over the edges of the bamboo sides. Unless she was asleep, I had missed her in the hotel.

I decided to get cleaned up now, then head back to the hotel. In the meantime, maybe Merci would show up so we could talk. I showered, shaved, and found a pair of dress slacks to wear with my khaki colored linen shirt.

I splashed cologne over my face, then changed everything from my short pockets into the slacks I was wearing. I picked up my keys and hurried outside to check on Merci.

Merci

I finished up my spa treatment with a manicure and a pedicure. I felt amazing, my hair was conditioned and soft, and I had nowhere to go. I was starving and decided to try out the beach bar on my own before I went back to my suite and got dressed. I was covered up enough; I'd seen many other guests sitting at the bar wearing less than I was.

I sat down at the bar and Sam hurried right over. "What can I get you, Merci? Ryan said anything you want to drink and eat is on the house."

"I'm starving, and I normally go for a salad, but at the moment, I'm craving meat."

Sam started choking. "Sam, are you okay?"

"Yeh, give me a minute. I've never heard anyone say that before." He coughed a few more times, then stepped back up to the bar. "What would you like, Doll?"

"I will take the burger and fries. I'm not sure what I want to drink with those. Can you make a suggestion? What is the best drink to have with meat?"

"Let me put your order into the computer, and I'll think of something. Wait right here."

Where else would I go, and why? This place was fantastic. The weather was perfect, there wasn't a cloud in the sky, and the ocean was throwing distance from where I sat.

"I've been trying out some of my pop's old drink recipes. This is a classic mojito with a twist. It should go great with your… uh, meat. Try it and tell me what you think. Your burger should be out in a few more minutes."

Sam set a large tropical looking glass in front of me, it had fresh pineapple, limes, and lemons on the side and it smelled minty. I took a sip, and I know my eyes rolled back into my head.

Sam set my burger in front of me and waited for me to bite into it. "How's your burger, is it cooked enough?"

I wiped at the juices running down my chin. "Always happens, thanks for asking while my mouth was full."

"Uh, honey, you don't know full." He laughed at his own joke before he asked about the drink.

"Well I've never had one before, so I don't have anything to compare it to, but it is wonderful. Thank you."

He tapped the bar, then said you are welcome before he went to help the two older gentlemen who had just sat down a few seats down from me.

~~

The burger had been delicious. That was one thing this place did right. I hadn't had anything that hadn't been prepared correctly. I pushed away half the burger and fries, and when Sam came to remove my plate.

"I'd like another Mojito if you don't mind. That was my first."

Sam grinned at me. "I like being a woman's first. Tell me what a beautiful woman like you usually drinks. I'm looking for inspiration."

"I'm not a drinker, but I do have experience with Fireball Whiskey. Only the shots. What other things can you do with that stuff?"

"I will think of something and name it after you."

"Sounds good, thanks, Sam."

"We'd like to buy the lady's next drink." I heard the two who had just sat down offer.

I almost told them that it was already taken care of, but decided it wouldn't hurt to have some fun with them. "Thank you so much. Sam, you heard them, another Mojito and they are buying."

Sam shook his head at me before he started preparing my drink.

Ryan

I'd spent precisely forty-five minutes getting ready; plenty of time for Merci to find her way back to her room. I knocked on her door and listened; still, nothing moving inside. I had the master key, but entering her place in the light of day seemed intrusive. Oh well, maybe she'd found a hole in the rocks somewhere to read a book. *I could only hope that was where she was.*

I was past the point of being irritated as I strolled back to the beach bar. Nothing had gone the way I'd wanted it to this afternoon. Hopefully, the evening's entertainment would put me in a better mood.

I heard her giggling before I actually saw her. A man was sitting next to her at the bar, and the sight of his hand on her bare thigh had me seeing red. I should have stopped and used any of the methods I'd used in the past to handle irate customers or possible lethal situations, but he had no right touching her leg.

"Excuse me, but this isn't that kind of establishment, you can take your business elsewhere." The statement I made could have been heard over the entire beach. Merci, who I considered at this time to be my woman was surrounded on both sides by older men who had no right touching her at all.

One of the two spoke up to defend the girl who he'd been groping. "Miss, I do believe he just insinuated that you are a whore. You had better apologize to her immediately, then find yourself another place to have a drink. My friend and I were enjoying this young lady's company, and you just made things get rather ugly."

"What did you say, Ryan? Are you talking to me, or to my friends? You sound just like a jealous schoolboy. I am not your property, I never was. You need to apologize to these two gentlemen and me."

"How much have you had to drink, Merci? I'm just looking out for your safety."

The other man sitting next to her stood up and moved in my direction. "You heard the lady, apologize then find somewhere else for your fun. We're taking good care of this sweet thing. Fuck off!"

I looked across the bar and saw Sam standing there with his Billy club. He kept that under the bar always in case an uncooperative customer became too drunk to reason with. "You heard Mr. West, you both need to leave. We'll make sure the young lady gets back to her room safely."

Both men stood up and backed away from their stools. "Last chance, sweetie. We can both show you a better time than this loser can."

"She's not going anywhere but back to her room. I've taken care of your tabs; please leave this establishment before I call the police and have you both removed." I watched them until they were out of sight, then I turned to look at Merci.

"You are an ass, Ryan! You are not my husband, boss, or father for heaven sake. Nor do you have the right to tell me who I can or can't see. I do believe those two gentlemen were right; you just implied that I was a whore. Didn't you? Ryan West, you sure do know how to cut someone deep."

She got off her bar stool, staggered just a little, then turned and smiled at Sam. "Thank you for your company, Sam."

I reached out and tried to take her hand. "Back off, buddy. I can find my own way back to the snake pit. You can stay here and guard your precious hotel and beach. Goodbye."

I stayed in the same spot watching her stumbling back to her suite.

"She sure is a pistol. I think you blew it, boss."

"I think you're right, Sam. I have no perception of right or wrong when she's involved. I hope I didn't ruin my chances to speak with her later. Thanks for keeping an eye on her for me. I should have known you'd never let anything happen to any of my guests."

"She's more than that; I can tell how much she means to you. You've got that deer in the headlight look whenever she's nearby. I've got a suggestion for you, boss. Next time, before you get the urge to approach her, take a few minutes and count to twenty. Ten isn't enough in her case."

"Thanks, I'll try to remember that."

Chapter Fifteen

Merci

I stumbled away from the bar angrier and more hurt than I'd ever been before. That man had no clue how much his words had wounded me. I'd never let him see me cry for him again. The way he'd treated me back there in front of Sam and the other two men had been very insulting. I think they were right, in a roundabout way he had accused me of being a hooker.

I knew the men wanted me to go with them to their rooms, and I also knew Sam had been watching every move they had made toward me. If their advances had become more aggressive, Sam would have gotten rid of them for me. I wasn't gullible enough to do something so stupid with two strangers after I'd been drinking.

I had gone back to Ryan's room with him the first time I'd gotten drunk on Fireball Whiskey. He'd been a stranger, and look what had happened to me since then. He had changed my life for the better. But did that give him the right to dictate to me now?

I was sobbing by the time I reached my room. If I saw another man with soft brown eyes, it would be too soon. I should avoid men with that eye color at all costs. Maybe I'd look for someone with blue eyes in the future. Someone who was opposite of Ryan and Paul.

Merci, you are an idiot. Just avoid all men period.

It was still early. I'd had the full spa treatment, I'd had lunch and drinks, and I'd had enough fun on the beach. What could I do to keep myself occupied now? Sitting all night in my hotel suite feeling sorry for myself wasn't an option for me either. I had no intentions of returning to the hotel where I might run into Ryan again.

I missed my two girls so much. It would be their nap time, and I'd already spoken to them once today so calling them again would just make my mother even more concerned for me.

It was only Thursday; I still had work to do tomorrow. I'd call Troy and ask him what time we were meeting in the morning. Jameron was taking me on a tour of the city on Saturday and dancing in the evening. If I could avoid any contact with Ryan for a few days, at least until I could figure out what I wanted to do about him then maybe I could make this work. I still had one more week to go after this one. I would never have guessed I'd be counting the days until I left paradise.

I called the hotel operator and asked her to connect me to Troy's room. I just couldn't remember which room number he was staying in. "Troy, this is Merci. How was your day? Do you know what our plans are for tomorrow? That sounds perfect; what time do you want me to meet you there in the morning?"

I listened to him go on and on about the place that, Ryan, was taking the entire group later on. "That sounds like something that I'm glad I wasn't invited to do. So I suppose that means I'm on my own this evening as well? Good to know; have a great time. I will let you sleep in in the morning; I'm sure after overindulging tonight you might need your beauty rest or recovery time. I will speak to you tomorrow."

I slowly hung up the phone. "Men are all sleazes; they would be happy for the rest of their lives if they just had half-naked women entertaining them and doing their bidding. Unless of course, they were like my ex, Paul. Then you'd want half-naked gorgeous men dancing for you." Society was all messed up. Why couldn't I find that one special man who was satisfied with me by his side forever?

It was a relief when I'd finally found out Paul was gay. I could never compete with another man for his attention, and somehow, I was okay with that. It was easier for me to accept than if he'd been sleeping with another woman. Competition with another female was painfully hard; especially when that other woman was carrying the man in question's child.

Ryan

I had just finished speaking to Jameron. We were all set, George and Douglas were already waiting in the limo with Troy. The Loft was a favorite place for male tourists but was only accessible if you knew someone who lived on the island. I'd discovered it the second time I'd come to St. Lucia with Tricia. We'd been in the middle of another one of our arguments, and Jameron had taken me there to meet his girlfriend, Lucy. That had been quite a few years back.

I climbed into the back seat with the others. "Good evening, are you ready for some island entertainment? Let me tell you a little bit more about The Loft before we get there. There are rules we must follow once we are inside, and anyone who is caught breaking any rule will be ejected and will never be allowed into the establishment again."

Troy asked, "Jameron, does Jasmine still run the place?"

"Yes, she does. Jasmine is a woman who is envied by her peers. She is brilliant when it comes to her business, and she has the best people working for her. Do as Ryan has told you or she will have you tossed outside by one of her Carpenters. Those are her enforcers;

they are like a bouncer, but they follow her rules. She doesn't want anything to happen to her girls. Keep your hands to yourselves unless you are invited to go into a private room with one of them. Also, remember to ask before you do or touch anything."

Jameron drove the limo up to the foliage covered path lined with decorative lights. He assisted all of us out of the car, then parked it just around the corner from where we stood. I wasn't going anywhere without him by my side. The first time I'd come on my own had been a colossal mistake.

We stayed close to him on the path which turned sharply, and from there we climbed a set of steep stairs which took us into the cozy building which was partially built into the top of a massive tree.

If Jasmine ever decided to sell the place, she could get a lot of money for this location. It was unique and offered the most exceptional types of performances from the women she had working for her.

I turned and spoke to my guests. "Gentlemen, prepare for the most extraordinary experience of your lives."

We followed Jameron into the dimly lit entrance of *The Hut*. I knew what to expect since I had been here more than once. Now I got more enjoyment from observing the faces of the guests that I brought with me than I did from watching the women perform. Tonight, I planned on getting drunk; I wanted to forget all about Tricia, and Merci.

We waited in the entrance for Jasmine to arrive. Jameron had called her from the Limo to let her know when we would be arriving. When she came through the door, she didn't disappoint us. Jasmine was almost six foot tall and very slender. She wore dark jasmine, almost purple colored contacts to change her eye color which is where she took her name from. I hadn't seen her without them and had always wondered what color they truly were. Her face was slender, and she had delicate features, especially for a woman her size. Her full mouth was permanently outlined with a dark lip liner, and she had bright red lip gloss on them now.

Her dark hair was intricately weaved with a lighter color of blond, and the pattern swirled around over the top of her skull, then flowed loosely down the center of her back. But the one unrivaled feature that she was most known for was her enormous breasts. She wore a colorful loose-fitting skirt under her dark blue blouse which was cut to show as much cleavage that she could without showing her nipples.

"Jameron Sebastián, it has been a long time. Where have you been hiding?" She threw her arms around the back of his neck and kissed him long and hard while the rest of us watched.

"It's nice to see you again, Jasmine. Let me introduce you to my friends. You already know Ryan West."

She approached me then reached for my hands. She leaned in closer to me and kissed the side of my mouth. "Mr. West, Jameron tells me you and your lovely wife are expecting. Congratulations. Why isn't she here with you celebrating?"

"It's nice to see you again, Jasmine. You are just as lovely as the last time I saw you. I came here to entertain my business contacts and not my wife. It's a male only night out. Let me introduce you to my business associate, Troy Masters. We've been friends for a long time."

Jasmine shook Troy's hand then smiled at me. "Now I know why your wife didn't come with you this evening. Mr. Masters, welcome."

Troy gave her a funny look after she made her observation, and I hid a smile. "This is Douglas Brandt and George Tanner. I hope to have them invest in my property before they leave the island in a few days. I brought them with me tonight for you to work your magic on them."

She welcomed them, and as she took each of their hands separately, she did what I called her party tricks and asked them about a specific person or event in their life. "George, be sure and call your wife later this evening and let her know when you will be coming home. She worries about you when you travel."

Then she took Doug's hand. "I have the feeling you will be spending more time on our island. Ryan, you have made some good choices. After meeting your guests, I have changed my selection of the girls who will be entertaining you and your guests. Please follow me; I will show you the best table in my establishment."

She took us to a large booth with high backed cushioned seats which were placed in a half circle around a table with a pole coming up through the center of it. The top of the pole looked like tree branches full of leaves and exotic flowers. There were only a few other tables like this one scattered around the room.

Jasmine had a beautiful full smile which she turned on us now. "Your server, Ashlyn will be right over to get your drink orders. Gentlemen, I hope you enjoy your evening."

Merci

I hadn't gotten myself really dressed up yet. I'd purchased the party dress that I wore just last night, and I had one in mind to wear when I went out with Jameron on Saturday. Tonight, there would be no chance of running into Ryan, Troy or Jameron. I wanted to get all fancied up and find my own entertainment for the night.

I decided to call the hotel desk and ask for recommendations. "Pheora, this is Merci Crandall; I'm staying in one of the beach suites. Could you tell me where I can go and either see a show or possibly find somewhere where there might be dancing or entertainment? I wanted to get dressed up this evening and celebrate." I listened to her recommendations. "That sounds like just what I was looking for. Is there a car that can take me into town, or should I call a taxi?"

After listening to her recommendations, I decided to make a trip to Rodney Bay. The girl at the front desk said that is where all the cruise ships were docked in the water, and there were more things to do there because of the tourists who would be arriving for the weekend. She said it was mostly casual, but once I got there, I might be able to find something to do that was a little more refined. She told me to call when I was ready to go, and she would either call a taxi for me or see if she could find a driver to take me there for the evening.

"Thank you so much for your help." Yay, I was going to go out on my own and have some fun. I decided she was probably right; I didn't want to get all dressed up for nothing. She said there was someplace in town that had street performances outside, but other than fine dining most people dressed more casual.

Oh well, I'd go casual then. I put on more makeup, brushed out my hair, then put on a short skirt made out of blue jean material, and put on a pink sleeveless button up shirt that I tied at the waist. I slipped on my pink sandals and called for a cab to pick me up in front of the hotel.

I applied my perfume, and lip gloss, and I ran out the door. I waved at Sam as I passed by him in the bar. I wondered if he ever had any time off. He'd be a lot of fun to go out with. I stopped and walked back to ask him.

"Hey, Sam. Do you work all the time?"

"Sometimes it feels like I do. You look pretty, have you got a date?"

"Thank you. I don't, but I wondered if you were getting off soon? Just thought I'd see if you wanted to go into town with me?"

"I'm off at seven, but I'm already meeting someone for dinner. Sorry. Where are you going to?"

"Nowhere in particular. Pheora told me about Rodney Bay. She said that's where all the tourists land from the cruise ships. Have a nice dinner; I will talk to you in the morning."

I heard him call out as I hurried away, "Be sure and call to let Ryan know where you are going."

"Yeah, right. I'm a big girl, and I can take care of myself."

The Island Runner Cab Company was waiting with a car in front of the hotel as soon as I stepped outside. I climbed into the back seat, and the driver asked where I was going.

"Take me to Rodney Bay. Find me the best place to have dinner, and just leave me with your phone number to call later when I need a ride back."

"Sure thing." He waited for me to close the door, then pulled the cab onto the highway. "Where are you from?"

"The Western United States. It's the first time I've ever been here. What would you recommend for me to do in town?"

He winked at me in the rear-view mirror. "I can think of a lot of things that I enjoy doing, but none of them would be good enough for a young woman such as yourself. I'll drop you off at the end of the main street. From there you can walk down to the beach. There's a lot of tourist traps, but there are some good places to eat and hang out to watch the local entertainment. You will have a good time there."

Danny parked on the side of the road at Reduit Beach Avenue, and pointed in different directions and told me which way to go for the different activities. He handed me his card and told me to call a half hour before I was ready for him to come back and pick me up.

"Thank you, Danny. I appreciate all your help."

"One more caution; stay away from the next street over. There is a nightclub that caters to rich old farts who would like nothing better than to find a young American blond female walking the streets all alone."

"Thanks for the warning. I will talk to you later." He pulled away from the curb, and I started down the street to begin my new tourist adventure, which I decided to call, *a dumb blond hooker on a mission to have fun in the streets of St. Lucia.*

"That's kind of a long title, wouldn't it sound better if you shortened it some?" I carried on the conversation with myself to relieve the nervousness I felt at being alone. When I first set out this evening on my own, I didn't think it would have bothered me so much. It did once Danny told me the story about the street filled with men looking for lone females. I was probably just fine all by myself, but his remark kept bothering me.

I decided to keep moving until I found somewhere that was overrun with lots of people. The old farts he spoke of would never catch me in a crowd, only if I were all alone.

Chapter Sixteen

Merci

I finally found a busy looking place that had live entertainment going on in the corner of the room. I noticed the backside of it from the street; it was open aired and backed up next to the ocean. The place was already popping with a diverse assortment of people.

The name in bold red letters on the side of the building said, *Reduit Rum Bar*, and in small letters below, *ocean fresh fun*. Okay then, I could try that. I loved shrimp, and something fruity and rummy from the bar sounded terrific.

I walked into the place, and the smells, as well as the sounds thrumming around me, assailed my senses. I pushed my way up to the bar and waited for the bartender to notice me standing there; there was nothing left for me to sit on.

"Excuse me, could I get a drink?"

Eli finally noticed me standing in the crowd and hurried over with an enormous grin on his gorgeous face. "What can I make for you, Miss."

I was tongue tied and stuttered on my words. "Th…They sure don't have guys who look as cute as you where I'm from."

He tossed his head back and laughed. "Flattery will get you your first drink on the house, but not your boyfriend's. Did he send you to the bar to get drinks on your own?"

"I'm not here with a boyfriend; I'm painting the town red on my own."

"Red now is it? What can I make you…?"

"Merci, my name is Merci. I'm not a rum drinker, but someone told me it makes the best fruity drinks. Why don't you surprise me with something icy, and delicious?"

"I will be right back, don't you leave from that spot, and if my partner over there tries to use the same lines on you that I already have, tell him Eli is taking care of you."

I couldn't help but giggle. I'd made the right decision to come here, my night was already improving, and the promise of more fun to come was a sure thing. I examined the crowd of people packed inside the small building; they wandered in, and out of the back doors continuously that went out onto the back patio. The band in the corner started playing their instruments once again, and a sexy young black woman stood up next to the piano and began singing the words to a popular song they were performing for the younger crowds.

Eli handed me a tall drink with a pineapple spear sticking out the top of it. "Rum punch, extra ice. Enjoy."

I sipped from the straw as I made my way outside. The place was filled with couples who were either dancing, talking or in some corners making out. But there were others just like myself who just wandered the area and watched. I squeezed through the door and stepped out onto the brightly decorated beach patio. The ocean was just feet away. The sun would be resting on the water soon before it disappeared for the night, and the view of the sunset from here would be spectacular.

The music was still quite loud outside, and fewer couples were dancing together. There was more of a mixed crowd dancing all together just where they stood. I was already feeling the rum punch, so when a gorgeous younger male stood in front of me and started dancing, I couldn't help myself from moving to the music with him.

He had a charming smile. "Are you having a nice night, miss?"

"Absolutely, and you?"

"With a beautiful woman close by, how could it get any better?"

We tried to chat with one another, but the music grew louder. Soon we could no longer hear what the other one was saying, so we just kept moving to the music. Eventually, I was dancing with an entire group of men. Three lighter-skinned blacks and one white man who was overly tanned and had blond curly hair. I also noticed a pretty, but much younger woman than I was dancing next to me. I'd finished my drink, and someone put another one in my hand.

I didn't notice when the lights grew dimmer; the music in the room had also changed its tempo. Ultimately, as the night went on, the area I danced in grew more crowded; the dancing became more sensuous and erotic. I became lost in the music; my moves became more daring and sexy.

Ryan

The young woman who danced around the pole at our table reminded me too much of Merci. Her name was Roxy, and she had a nice ass. Jasmine was indeed a witch; she saw too much in her visions when she spoke with her customers. She had known exactly who it was that I was looking for when I sat down, and she had provided the right dancer to entertain me.

Both Douglas and George had already spent time in one of the private caves with a dancer, and I hadn't seen Troy for an hour or more. I'd lost track of the number of drinks that I'd had, but I'd stayed seated the entire night at this table with Jameron.

Jameron leaned over and whispered, "I hope we don't have to carry, George, to the car. How are you doing my friend?" He gestured at the girl who now was almost completely nude in front of us. "Have you had a chance to speak to Merci yet? I wanted to let her know we would be gone for the evening and to stay close to the hotel, but I never got a chance. Have you had a chance to check on her yet?"

"She was pretty toasted the last time I spoke to her. I'm sure she'll probably stay in her room and watch TV. Besides, I believe it's my turn for a dance next." I stood up from the table and took the dancers hand in front of me to stop Jameron from reminding me of the reason I had come here, to begin with. Roxy climbed off the table, and I noticed up close how haggard her face was. Still, I followed her into one of the small, secluded caves for my own private show. At this point I didn't care who she looked like, I just wanted to forget.

I knew what the rules were in the caves, but Roxy it seemed wanted to bend them. As the music continued, her movements became almost vulgar. Or maybe it only seemed that way. I knew she wasn't what I needed or wanted any more. I decided to stay until she was finished to be polite.

Jameron burst into the room with Jasmine on his heels. "Ryan, we must leave. Merci left the hotel some time ago, and she hasn't been heard from since. She shouldn't be alone anywhere on the island. There is too much that could happen to someone who looks like her."

"Merci? Christ, why couldn't she just stay in her room like a good girl?"

Jameron was angry when he answered me. "She is a good girl, and that is the problem. She will be hurt. Jasmine called a cab to take George and Donald back to the hotel. She has one of her girls searching for Troy now."

"Jam, should we send Troy back to the hotel with Donald and George?"

"We don't know where Merci is, but if she is in trouble, we might need his help."

"What if she isn't? What if she is sitting at the movie theater watching a chick flick."

Jasmine spoke next, and the hair on my arms stood on end. "Your pretty blond woman is in a room full of strangers. She isn't alone, but she could be in trouble. I sense that her mind is fuzzy. She is drinking too much, but something else is in her drink. She may have been drugged."

I grabbed onto Jasmine's arm. "Where is she? Is she nearby or on the other side of the island, can you tell, Jasmine?"

"She is close; I wouldn't feel her if she was far away. She is still dancing, but she is fading fast. Find the music, hurry Jameron. Hurry!"

"There is no time to call a cab, let's go!" We both ran for the door, and I saw Troy leaning up against the bar. "Troy, Merci is in trouble. Can you still walk?"

"Shit, where is she?" Troy sobered up quickly when he heard me say that.

"We only know she is somewhere near here dancing; we've got to find her on foot."

Merci

I felt like I was floating on air. I didn't have a care in the world; I was having such a remarkable time dancing with my new friends. I noticed that everyone surrounding me was slippery and drenched in sweat; when had the room become so crowded? The room began to spin around me, I felt hot and muzzy.

I heard a man's voice from behind me say, "I've got you sweetness, just lean back, I won't let you fall."

"No, I won't fall." I felt his hands on my waist, and his friend who was moving in front of me smiled then pushed one of his legs in between my knees.

"What is your name, lovely? Who did you come with?"

"You help me stay up too? You are so nice. No, I'm not lovely, I'm…my name is…Merci. You have a nice smile. Do you know Jam, he has a nice smile too, and so does…so does…"

"Merci, you are hot, would you like another drink? Eli, another drink for this sweet thing."

"No, Eli, jes some water. No more rum punch."

"Would you like to get some fresh air, sweetness? Bede, help me get her outback for some fresh air."

"Fresh air, uh hum. I need fresh air; everything is blurry. Maybe I need somethin to eat. Can Eli get me somethin to eat?"

"We've all got something to feed you, sweetness. Bede, she's slipping, pick her up."

"No, I can walk. Wait, don't pick me up I might fall." The hands around my waist became rougher as I was lifted into the air and tossed over someone's shoulder. The next thing I knew I was hanging upside down with my face brushing up against the back of a sweaty t-shirt. I felt sick. The hand holding my legs ran up my leg and squeezed my butt. I tried to tell him to stop. My head was pounding against the man's back as he carried me out the door. I heard laughter as I fought to stay awake.

Ryan

Jameron had the right frame of mind to call the local police. We didn't know what Merci had been wearing when she went out for the evening, but we could describe her. Jameron also got a call back from the hotel. Pheora had been at the front desk when Merci had called earlier asking for some suggestions of places to visit in the city. She had given her the number for a cab company, and she read it to me. I jotted it down then handed the number to Troy and asked him to track down the driver who brought her out here.

"I've got it. Danny is the driver who drove her out here; he is on his way back now. He dropped her off at the top of the street on Reduit Beach Avenue. He gave her his number to call him when she was ready to leave, but he hasn't heard from her yet. He was on his way back here to look for her."

Jameron called the police back and told them where she had been dropped off, and we made our way over to that street. "When I find her, I'm going to make her pack her things and leave. I can't take this anymore."

"What about your wife, Ryan. Have you considered her feelings? What do you think she will do when she finds out how much this girl means to you?"

I didn't want to argue with him about Tricia. "Troy, I don't have time for this right now, but soon. We are all going to sit down and talk. You, Tricia and I."

"Ryan, look down there near the end of this block. See them? There is a group of men coming out of that club down the street. That must be Merci that is being carried. I'll let the police know which way they are going. I think we have found her."

Jameron was correct; I saw Merci's beautiful blond hair brushing across the ground. "Yes, I'm sure that's her; we can't wait for the police. Jameron, they could have a car close by to put her in. We've got to stop them!"

Troy and I started running down the street, the men who had Merci had turned the corner, and we could no longer see her.

A taxi pulled up next to us. "Get in, hurry." We all jumped inside the taxi, and he drove to the corner where we saw her disappear.

"There she is, hurry up and get out of the car! Troy, you run that way, and I'll go on this side. Jameron, how close are the police?"

As soon as I asked, we heard the sirens and then a couple of police cars pulled in front of the van as it turned out onto the street. The officers jumped out of their cars with their guns drawn and yelled for whoever was inside the van get out and put their hands straight up.

Jameron held onto my arm to stop me from moving forward. Soon they had four men and one woman on the ground in handcuffs.

As soon as I knew it was safe for Merci, I ran into the van after a police officer to find her.

She was lying in a pile of filthy rags, her skirt was pushed up around her waist, but her panties were still on. Her blouse had been torn open, and I rushed over to her side and pulled her top shut to save her any further embarrassment. "Merci, I'm here, Darlin'. I almost lost you, and it won't happen again." She was out cold; whatever she had been given had knocked her out.

Jameron and Troy entered the van and helped me lift her up. "Call an ambulance. I don't know what she was given earlier, but she isn't moving. I want someone to look at her and make sure she is all right."

Jameron's tone of voice was as relieved as mine when he spoke. "They are on their way. She will be okay, Ryan. We found her in time, and she is safe."

"Thanks to you, Jameron. If you hadn't called and checked on her when you did, she would be gone. I can't think about that right now. I will send something to Jasmine to thank her for her help."

I heard another set of sirens outside of the van, and I carried Merci out with Troy's help. "I'm going with her to the hospital."

The ambulance attendant asked, "Are you a family member?"

Jameron answered for me. "Yes, he is. We will see you back at the hotel, Ryan. Please call and let us know how she is doing."

I nodded then got Troy's attention as they strapped Merci into the back of the ambulance. "Will you keep an eye on Tricia for me? Tell her I will explain everything to her later."

"Take care of Merci, Ryan. I'll be there with Patricia."

Chapter Seventeen

Merci

"Miss Crandall, it's nice to see you are back with the living. I'll leave you in the capable hands of your fiancé while I go and tell the doctor you are waking up. Can I get you anything while I'm gone, Mr. West?"

My head was pounding. I tried to open my eyes, but they felt glued shut. Where was I, and how did I get here. Were my girls here with me?

"Maddie, Allie, where are you?" I began to panic; I couldn't find them.

"Merci, it's okay, Darlin'. You're all right now. Hush, I'll call the doctor. You know you've had us all worried?"

"What happened, was I in an accident? Ryan, where am I?"

"Can you open your beautiful eyes and look at me, Merci? Let me see those pretty blues."

It was a struggle, but I opened them to see the face of the man I loved gazing down at me. "Ryan, you've got such a nice smile. Hmm, where am I, are my girls here? I want to see them and make sure they are okay."

"Your girls are home safe with your mom and dad, Merci. They are just fine. I spoke with them earlier; they wanted me to give you a kiss from them."

"My girls said that?"

"Yes, and so did your mom and dad. I must keep my promise." He bent down over the bed and kissed me softly on the cheek closest to him. "I told your parents I would have you call them as soon as the doctor releases you from the hospital."

"That wasn't much of a kiss coming from a fiancé. Why am I in the hospital, Ryan?"

"Don't you remember? I'll wait for the doctor to get here so he can explain what happened to you. I'm just glad to hear your voice again and see your lovely smile. I thought I'd lost you for good."

"I thought I'd lost you too, Ryan. Wait, where am I?"

I heard a loud voice answer from the door, "You are in the Tapion hospital, and your fiancé is correct, we thought we **had** lost you. You gave us quite a scare young lady."

A tall blond older man with kind green eyes sat down in the chair that Ryan had just vacated. "What I still don't understand is why you were alone in that club. Your fiancé says he was at a business meeting and didn't know you were going out on your own. You were lucky that he found you when he did."

"I still don't understand what happened, can one of you tell me why I am here?"

"Young lady, you were given an excessive amount of the drug Ketamine. It was probably put in your drink. Apparently, from the reports I have here, you didn't have much food in your system, and that drug works fast. Whoever gave it to you put enough of it in your drink to knock out a large man; as small as you are, we didn't know if we were going save you or not. Your fiancé has been by your side since they brought you in here. I believe he willed you to stay alive."

The doctor got up from the chair. "I will let him tell you the rest of the story. The police will be here soon to question you about the men who had you. I already let them know that you might not remember much that happened yet. But the good news is they didn't sexually assault you; things could have been much worse for you. I will talk to you in a few minutes."

I waited for the doctor to leave the room, then turned to look at Ryan. "When did you become my fiancé? I am so confused; the last thing I can remember was that you and your wife were expecting a baby. How long have I been in the hospital and where in the world is Tapion?"

Ryan

I leaned forward and kissed Merci on the forehead. "Tapion is in St. Lucia. You've been in the hospital for three days. Do you remember anything that happened to you since you've been here?"

Merci's face was so revealing when she was trying to figure things out. She was confused and probably didn't remember much of anything that happened to her on the night the doctor had admitted her to the hospital. I wanted to know for myself that whoever had been with her in the club hadn't done something to her while she was there. But if they had maybe I was best that she forgot.

"St. Lucia? I still don't remember when you became my fiancé?"

"I'm not, but it was the only way they would let me stay here with you, Merci. I couldn't let you be in here all alone. I'm not your fiancé, but we do have a lot to talk about when you are better. As far as my wife having a child, she is, but that is another long story for another day. Right now, you just need to focus on your recovery, so I can get you out of here and take you back to the hotel."

"Ryan, you said you spoke to my girls and with my parents? Did you tell them what happened to me to put me in the hospital? Oh my gosh, my mom must be out of her mind with worry."

"No, Merci. I didn't tell them why you were here, just that you had a little accident. Don't worry, they spoke to the doctor, and he assured them you would fully recover and that it wasn't life-threatening. But it could have been. You probably won't remember most of that night, and the doctor told me you could have flashbacks. I want to know why in the hell you decided it was okay to go into town on your own. Merci, why would you do that, don't you know anything about how dangerous it is for beautiful young girls to be alone in a foreign country?"

"No, I don't remember why I was out on my own. I was probably upset at something; that's the only reason I can think of that would make me do something stupid. I must have had something on my mind other than my safety. Could it have been you who got me upset, Ryan?"

Everything that happened to Merci was my fault; I had hurt her earlier in the evening. But I didn't want to bring that up with her now. "I've screwed things up left and right when it comes to you, Merci. Like I said before, we've got a lot to discuss once you are out of here. Right now, I just want to look at you and thank our mutual friend, Jameron for a hunch he had while he and I were out together. You are safe now, and generally unharmed."

"Well then, I'm glad I'm getting better. I can't wait to have a burger with french fries. I think I was dreaming about them before I woke up. Did you hear my stomach growling?"

I tossed my head back and laughed. Merci seemed like she was her old self again, and even better, she didn't remember what an asshole I was yet. "You are lucky. I know someone who can arrange that. I might ask, Jameron, to sneak one in for you while you are here. That reminds me, I promised a few people I would call as soon as you woke up. I'll be right back; don't you dare go anywhere while I'm gone. I'm not going to lose you again."

I left her room and closed the door. The first person I called was Jameron. "Merci is awake, and she doesn't remember anything that happened to her yet. In a way, I hope she never does. The police are on their way to question her now. After that, it shouldn't be too much longer before the doctor releases her."

"Will you let Troy know. He can tell Tricia whatever he wants to. I'm sure she knows by now that we are no longer a couple and I am tired of her lies. I will call you when Merci is ready to be released. I've got one more phone call to make. Did our guests make their flight home this morning? Good, thank you for all your help, Jameron. Talk to you soon. Yes, I will tell her. Goodbye."

I pushed the button to disconnect the phone call with Jameron. I promised Merci's father I would call him as soon as she woke up. I had also promised him I would do the right thing as far as she and I were concerned.

I picked up the phone and made call I dreaded. "Mr. Lachance, Merci is awake. She seems to be doing okay. She still has some memory loss which might be a good thing considering what she went through. I haven't said anything to her yet, but I will as soon as we get back to my hotel. Yes, sir. I already told her I would have her call you as soon as we get back."

Merci

I tried to stay focused on Ryan as he moved around the room. My head hurt more when I tried to remember anything from the night in question; for me, it was better to sit and listen and observe. Ryan mentioned that my memory might come back in flashbacks. What had happened to me? I guessed when I was ready to remember; I would.

Waking up to find Ryan by my side had made me very happy. I loved the man so much it hurt, and he seemed to have feelings for me still as well. But just like before, until we discussed his wife and child, our feelings for each other couldn't go any further. I wasn't going to be a home wrecker.

Ryan walked back into the room with a scowl on his face. "Oh no, is everything all right?"

His eyes met mine. His look said more than his words ever could. "Everything will be just fine, Merci. I will make sure of it. Do you remember what you asked me earlier? It had to do with a fiancé and the kisses he gave his woman. I haven't given you a proper kiss in weeks. I'd like to make up for that as soon as possible, but this one will have to suffice until then."

Ryan sat down on the bed next to me; he caressed my face then smoothed the hair away from my face. He leaned in closer to whisper in my ear. "You stink, and I intend to treat you to a hot bubble bath as soon as I get you back to my suite."

I smacked the top of his hand. "That wasn't a very nice thing to say to me. But you are right; I do stink, and so do you, Mr. West. A hot bubble bath sounds amazing. I'm looking forward to soaking in the tub."

"It will be my pleasure, Darlin'."

It wasn't my idea of the perfect setting for a kiss, but beggars can't be choosers. Ryan still smiled as he slowly lowered his lips to cover mine. Neither one of us moved after his lips locked onto my mouth. He kept them there for only a few seconds, before lifting his head and smiling. "I adore you, Merci. I don't know if I've ever told you that, but I do."

We both heard the doctor clear his throat from the doorway. "The police have some questions for Merci. They asked if you would leave the room, so they can get more honest answers. When your fiancé returns, we can talk about your release."

Ryan reached for my hand and squeezed. "I will be outside the door waiting. I can't wait to get you out of here."

Two police officers moved closer to the bed, and one of them started asking me questions. "The Doctor told us you were given a large dose of Ketamine. That is a date rape drug, and it acts very fast in the system; it has many other side effects as well. We were hoping for any details from the night the incident occurred. Who were you with, what time did you arrive at that club, and when did you remember feeling like something was wrong? Can you give us any names or descriptions of the people who were around you or did you notice someone who was paying extra attention to you, or seemed to watch you closely? We've had similar things happen in this area; this is the closest we've come to finding out who else might be involved. Miss Crandall, any little detail could help."

"I know this might sound odd, but I don't remember anything about where I was, or who I was with, yet. I would very much like to help you, but until my memory comes back, I can't."

"One more question, did you have someone else with you who might know something?"

"I'm sorry, but the last thing I remembered when I woke was walking on the beach. I don't know what day that was or anything else right now. The doctor did tell me that I might have my memory come back in flashbacks. Can I call you if I think of something?"

"Here is the card with the number to call. Please, even if it seems incidental to you, it might be the lead we are looking for to solve this and many other cases. Thank you, Miss Crandall."

They both left my room. After being questioned by them I became even more concerned as to what had happened to me. If the police were investigating, it must have been quite dangerous. Ryan must know something; I could hear his muffled voice talking with the officers just outside my door.

Ryan

"We were notified that Miss Crandall; your fiancé had gone out on her own by the cab driver who dropped her off on the street. Can you tell us where you were, and did you know where she was going too?"

I hated giving out my personal information to anyone. Even though these two men were officers, I was still big news on this island. "Merci and I had a difference of opinion earlier in the evening; I suppose she wanted some time alone."

"Where were you when this happened to her? We also want to know who you were with and is there anyone who can verify your story." The officer questioning me was just a young pup. He didn't seem to believe what I was telling him. He'd be even more surprised once I told him where I had been. Who in their right mind would leave someone who looked like Merci, and visit a gentlemen's strip club without her?

"I took a few prospective investors and my colleagues and me to *The Hut*. The proprietor, Jasmine can vouch for us all. We left there when my general manager called my hotel to check on the well-being of Miss Crandall. She wasn't feeling well earlier and I hadn't expected her to leave the premises at all that night."

"What was your argument about?"

"You must already know the answer to that question. We did have a few unkind words to say to one another, but that was all it was."

"According to one of your employees, it was more than just a few unkind words. We also discovered that you chased a few of your guests from the property. Could one of them be involved in her abduction? You know, to get back at you for ruining their plans with the young lady? Just one more question for you, Mr. West." Mr. hot shot cop smirked.

"And what could that be? You are wasting my time and yours with this line of questioning."

"Mr. West, do you often bring your wife and your fiancé to the same hotel on vacation?"

Now the little prick had really irritated the hell out of me. "It's complicated; one has nothing to do with the other."

The young officer who had done most of the talking cocked his head to the side, and the other one standing behind him sniggered. "Obviously. Here is my card, please call if you remember anything else that might help us with this case. Thank you, Mr. West."

I waited until they were no longer in sight, then rushed into the hospital room to find out that Merci had fallen back to sleep. I moved over to the bed and softly traced my finger over her full mouth. She was such an innocent, and this wouldn't have happened to her if I had only apologized to her that afternoon instead of inferring she was a whore at the bar.

The doctor entered the room behind me. "Mr. West, you can take Merci with you as soon as she wakes up. She is going to have one heck of a headache for the next few days. I'll give you a script for pain meds before you leave. She still might suffer dizzy spells as well as confusion; if it doesn't stop after a few days, bring her back to the hospital, and I will run some more tests on her."

"Thank you, doctor. I will do that." Now I needed to make my plans to get her back to the hotel and care for her without anyone else knowing she was there. I needed time alone with Merci to tell her how I felt, and to explain more about my plans for my life. She would sit still and listen to me tonight; I'd make sure of it.

Chapter Eighteen

Ryan

I called Jameron and asked him to prepare one of the penthouses for Merci and I. I also told him I didn't want any of the staff to know I would be there. I wanted nothing of this to reach Troy or Tricia. I asked Jameron to get everything ready for Merci and me; then he was to come to the hospital and help me get Merci back to the hotel.

"Merci, are you ready to get out of this joint? I've got plans for you when we return to my hotel."

"Hmm, that sounds wonderful. I hope there is food on the menu; I am starving."

I couldn't help myself from grinning. "I'm sorry, I did promise you a burger and fries. Those officers interfered with my plans to feed you. Don't worry; I will stuff you before I ravish you. I think a phone call to your parents and your girls should happen first. As soon as I get you safely in the backseat of the Limo, you can call them and let them know you are okay."

"I still can't believe you spoke to them. Who did you say you were?"

I wasn't ready to tell her about the entire conversation just yet, but lucky for me Jameron arrived in time to save me from an awkward conversation.

"Merci, how are you doing, girl?" Jam walked into the room and bent down to kiss Merci's cheek. "You had us worried. We are going to have a long discussion about the dangers of traipsing about an island full of hot-blooded young males alone. But for now, I am just here to take you and Ryan back to the hotel."

"Thank you, Jameron. It sounds like I am lucky to be here still. I would like to hear that discussion sometime, maybe after I remember what I did to deserve it first. I need some help getting out of this bed."

"Jam, can you get her from that side, and I will help her get up over here. Once we get downstairs, her doctor wants us to pick up her scripts along with his instructions from the reception desk. I'm ready when you are." I counted to three, and we both lifted Merci up from the hospital bed, then I mostly assisted her to the wheelchair.

"Hospital rules, you can't walk on your own anyway, I know you are still unsteady on your feet. Jam, I'll push, and you can get the elevator."

We made it to the first floor; then I pushed her out of the elevator and over to the reception desk. "We need the release papers for Merci Crandall, and the prescription the doctor was leaving for her as well. Is there a pharmacy in the hospital where I can fill it?"

~~

As soon as we picked up her pain medicine, we left for the hotel. There was a side entrance that our guests who wanted to remain incognito used when they stayed with us in the penthouse suites. I asked Jameron to take me to that door; then he could help me get Merci upstairs.

"I can't wait to get to that room. I need to apologize to both of you. Boy do I stink, and I'm sorry you two had to put up with me on the drive back."

Jameron was always a gentleman, which was one of the reasons I hired him to begin with. "Merci, with your beauty, how would anyone notice your smell. But, I will admit after a few days in a hospital, even you could use a shower." Jameron started laughing; then he winked at Merci from the front seat of the Limo.

"But, Ryan smells as if he'd wrestled with an entire team of soccer players. He needs a shower worse than you do."

"Thanks a lot, Jam. I suppose you're right. I'm ready for food and a shower as soon as I get Merci taken care of and bathed. Can you handle things in the meantime?"

"You will not be disturbed unless there is an emergency."

Merci

I enjoyed listening to the two of them tease one another. I was still very attracted to Jameron, and I knew Ryan was aware of that. But my heart belonged to Ryan.

"Hmm, a bath sounds absolutely amazing, Ryan. Perhaps you can ask for some cold grapes that you could feed me while I soak. Or perhaps, french fries. I know there is somewhere here that serves the best french fries in town. Give me a minute, and I'll remember which place it is."

"The food all comes from the same kitchen, so if it's fries that you want, you've got it."

We made it back to the hotel. Jameron climbed out of the front seat and hurried around the side of the limo to help Ryan get me out. "Thanks, guys. I'm still a bit woozy. I'm sure I'll feel much better with some food and water in me."

We entered the penthouse that I had been in once before. Ryan thanked Jam for his help, then closed the door. "He will order room service for us as soon as he parks the car. In the meantime, I can assist you into the bathroom."

I was nervous. I knew what Ryan wanted to do to me, but suddenly I didn't know if I was ready for the next step in our relationship or not. I still wasn't sure if we even had a relationship.

"Now that I am sitting down in a steady chair, can we try calling my family again? I'd feel a lot better hearing my girl's voices." It also gave me time to think about what was coming next.

"Of course, Merci. Here's the phone, dial the front desk and give them your phone number while I prepare our bath."

I waited until he left the room, then took a deep breath to calm myself. "Our bath, not my bath, or your bath, but our bath. Okay then." Ryan and I had bathed together before, it's not like he hadn't seen me naked, but I was still nervous. "Maybe what you need is a great big boa constrictor to put you in the mood." I picked up the phone and gave the girl at the front desk my parent's phone number.

"Mommy!"

I started to cry when I heard them yell my name. "Hello, Maddie, can you put it on speaker phone, so I can hear you both?" I waited until I could hear my parents talking in the background.

Then I heard Allie say, 'Maddie, I want to talk to mommy too.' 'She can hear you now, Allie, just say something."

"Hello, how are my big girls? I miss you both so much."

My mom yelled out, so I could hear her, "How are you feeling, Merci? That young man told us you had an accident. Are you, all right?"

"I'm just fine, mom. I just called to let you know I am back at the hotel. Ryan is going to make sure I eat something before I rest again. I can't wait to see you all. Dad, would you give mom a hug and tell her I am okay. Maddie, will you give Allie a big hug for me too. Girls, I will see you very soon."

Then I heard my father ask, "We want to know more about your, Ryan, when you get home. He promised me he would tell me everything when he brought you back. Tell him I am counting on it."

Oh great, what had Ryan told them? "I will. Have a good night. I'm going to hang up; I think room service is here with my dinner. I love you all so much."

"We love you too!" My family called out to me just before I disconnected the line.

"I suppose I'd better tell you what your father and I spoke about while you were in the hospital. But first, our dinner is here. After that, I can't wait to get you inside that tub."

Ryan

I caught the end of her conversation with her family. Merci loved her family. There was nothing mean or sarcastic when they spoke with one another. I'd never had that with my parents. After my discussion with her father, I knew how much they adored their daughter too. I also knew I needed to make things right between us before I met her family.

I opened the door and wheeled in the cart. "Merci, I should have asked. Would you like to eat first, or would you like to get cleaned up?"

She was avoiding my eyes. "Merci, if you need some more time we can eat. I don't want to hurt you, I do want to be with you, and **only** you. Trust that and me. Let me get you a plate of food first. Burger and fries, plus grapes. We can have the grapes in the tub as you suggested."

"Ryan, I don't know if I'm ready for this to happen yet. I've had many discriminating expectations of you in the past. Maybe I wasn't fair to you. But, the last time I thought we'd be together after the dance you and I had, you hurt me. Here on the island, it's been up and down and down and up between us the entire time I've been here. I think I need more time to get used to the idea of…us."

"Merci, I don't want to push you into anything. Darlin', I want to bathe with you so bad I hurt. But I also don't want to push you into doing anything that you aren't ready for. Eat your food; then I will help you get into the tub, alone if that's what you want. After you are finished bathing, I will jump into the shower. Does that sound okay to you for now?"

She smiled, and my heart melted a little bit more. "Thank you, Ryan. Who knows, once I'm in the tub I might change my mind. This burger smells so much better than I do. Did you get yourself one?"

I chuckled. "Yes, and boy am I glad I did. If I'm not going to eat you tonight, then I'll settle for the burger and fries."

She blushed, and I laughed even harder. "Merci, you do things to me…I wish…no I don't. Wait, yes, I do but not until you are ready. Eat your food, Merci."

She ate half her burger and a few of the fries while I devoured mine, then I started on the rest of hers. I handed her a bottle of water and grabbed the cold beer for myself. "Plying you with alcohol is out of the question for now. You've got to take some pain meds after your bath, and you don't need anything else screwing up your system. Here give me your plate."

In a softer, shyer voice, Merci answered me, "Thanks, Ryan. I'm ready for that bath now."

I sucked in a deep breath. "So am I. Take my hand, Merci."

I led her into the large bathroom, the mirrors scattered around the room were all covered in steam. I released her hand and walked forward to test the water. "It's still nice and hot. Merci, let me help you out of your clothes."

"Uh, okay."

"Don't worry; I'm not doing anything you don't want me to do. Here, give me your hand. Now kick off your shoes." I waited until her shoes were off, then I unbuttoned her pink shirt and pulled it slowly off her shoulders. Next, I unzipped her little blue skirt and slid it down her long silky legs.

She stood there in her white thong panties and matching lace bra. I wanted to devour her through the lacy material. Instead, I took another sketchy breath and reached behind her to unclasp her bra. I pulled it down deliberately over her arms, then dropped it in the pile of clothes on the floor next to me. I slipped a finger on either side of her panties and pulled them slowly down over her hips. Then I let them drop to the floor below her.

I couldn't help but devour her with my eyes. "My God, Merci. Even with you stinking to high heaven, I want to wrap myself around you and get lost."

"Very funny, Ryan. I'm cold, just help me get into that tub; it had better be perfumed, I don't want no stinking blond in my bed tonight."

"God almighty, you do wicked things to me." I slipped my arm under her knees and lifted her into the air, then I carried Merci over to the tub and carefully put her down into the steaming, frothy water.

Merci quickly sat down sloshing some of the sudsy water over the edge. She chuckled, and I just about wet the rest of my pants from the expressive sound.

"Now that I'm in here I feel so bad that you can't join me. Could you maybe wash my back?" She looked up at me through her long fluttering lashes then started laughing.

"If you don't stop that behavior right now, I won't be held responsible for my actions. I'll wash your back, then I'm going to put myself in a cold shower and hope you feel sorry for me."

Merci

I wish I were braver than I was; I enjoyed the responses I got when I teased Ryan. I loved that he was older than I was, more experienced and so eager to share…He had so much to teach me, and I couldn't wait to learn. But, tonight wasn't the right time for that. Not the way my head was feeling, and not until we discussed everything that was happening or not in his life.

Ryan pulled off his shirt, then got down on his knees next to the oversized tub. He reached for one of the wash clothes folded on a stack at the end of the tub in front of me, then pushed it under the water as he stared into my eyes.

In a raspy voice that I knew I was responsible for he asked, "Is the water hot enough for you, Merci?"

I just nodded my head up and down and turned around in the water, so he could reach my back. "Yes, it feels perfect. Do you want me to move forward a little bit more, so you can reach lower?"

"Are you trying to kill me? If I put my hand any lower into the water, don't be surprised to feel my fingers pushing their way into your gorgeous ass. Face the wall, Merci, and don't move."

I heard splashing behind me, then Ryan rubbed the cloth across my skin almost painfully. "Shit!" He had dropped the washcloth into the water. He swore again then stood up. "I'll be in my cold shower, call if you need me."

"Ryan, is everything all right?"

"No, it isn't. I'll hurry and wash up, then I'll be back to help you get out of the tub. I don't want you to slip and fall. I don't need any more shit from some small-town doctor about my fiancé or my wife."

"Wh…what do you mean by that?"

"Don't worry about it, Merci. I'll be out in a few minutes. Please don't pass out and slide under the water."

I stayed facing the wall until I heard the shower door shut, then I waited for the sound of the water to turn on. "Phew, he is driving me crazy. Now how do I get out of this tub and keep things cool between us?"

I quickly finished washing, then I turned on the warm water and got my hair wet from the tap. I didn't see any shampoo, and there was no way I was going to ask him to get me some while he was in the shower. I started laughing; we were acting just like a couple of horny teenagers who didn't want to get caught. The whole situation was my fault.

I waited until I heard the shower turn off. "Ryan, do you have any shampoo?"

I heard him mutter under his breath, "Jesus Christ, I can't take any more." Then he walked over to the side of the tub with a towel wrapped half-assed around his waist and glared as he handed me the bottle he'd grabbed from the counter.

I bit the inside of my lips to stop from laughing out loud at the look on his face. "I hate to ask but would you help me with my hair? It's so thick, and it'd hard to handle, and I…"

Then Ryan threw his head back and laughed with me. "You are talking about your hair and not something else now, right?"

That did it, I glanced at his towel, and I knew exactly what he meant. "Never mind, I will do it myself. Will you please wait outside the bathroom door until I call you?"

"I'll arrange for some clean clothes to be brought up here for you to put on. Hurry, I've got somewhere else that I need to be."

"Well, that was mean and hurtful. Really hurtful. Ryan West, why do I keep letting you hurt me so easily?" I was glad that I hadn't let things go any further than they had. How quickly he was able to dismiss me when he didn't get his own way.

I finished washing and rinsing my hair, then carefully climbed out of the shower and wrapped myself tightly with a few of the towels before I went to the door to wait for him to bring something back for me to put wear. I was done, finished, and ultimately heartbroken over what had occurred, or rather, hadn't in this bathroom.

Chapter Nineteen

Merci

Jameron had promised me a trip to Gros Islet Village on the weekend I ended up in the hospital. Today, we weren't going to go dancing, but he was excited to show me a better part of St. Lucia than I had been to before, so I agreed to go. I still hadn't heard anything from Ryan since he dropped me off at my suite after my bath. He'd sent Jameron up with my clothes, I got dressed, and he met me downstairs and walked me back to my room. That was the last time I had seen or heard from him.

I heard knocking outside of my door and opened it. Jameron stood there grinning from ear to ear. "Merci, are you sure you won't consider my previous offer. I would love a chance to get to know you better." He stepped into the room and pulled me in close to him.

"Merci, if I don't get this out of the way now, we will never make it in time to catch the tour bus into the city." He lowered his head and moved his lips slowly across mine. I opened my mouth willingly and followed his lead. His tongue moved slowly, and deftly through my mouth. Then he pulled back slightly, and I felt his smile on my lips.

"Jameron, you sure know how to make a girl swoon." I giggled. "That means take her breath away. And before you ask, yes, I am breathless. Aren't we waiting for a bus?"

"Yes, come sweetness, you need a hat and your purse. What is wrong, Merci? You are pale as a ghost."

"I just thought of something. When you called me sweetness, I remembered something from the other night. On our way through the hotel, I must tell Ryan what I remembered so he can call the police and let them know."

"Of course, Merci. I am sorry if it upset you."

"No, it's a good thing. I still don't know what happened to me, but every little bit will help me remember and possibly help the police find whoever else was responsible. Wait right here; I will ask where he is."

I knew he was in the hotel somewhere. I approached the girl at the front desk. "I need to speak with Ryan West, could you tell me where he is?"

"Yes, of course. He left a message saying he would be in his wife's suite. It's on the first floor up from the lobby. Room 119S."

"Thank you so much." His wife's room, maybe he was still trying to explain to her what had happened the other night when he went to the city. I took the elevator up and made my way down the hall. I counted the rooms as I made my way down the hall. Hers was straight ahead. I heard shouting coming from inside the room once I got there. I pressed my ear up against the door and listened for just a minute to what the two of them were arguing about.

The words coming from inside the room sounded muffled but clear as mud I heard Tricia and Ryan talking. Tricia asked, "Wait one minute, is she the whore who came to our door that night at your hotel? I knew she looked familiar."

It was Ryan's answer that hurt the most. "Yes, Merci was the whore who knocked on our door."

I didn't wait to hear any more of their conversation. I ran down the hallway and pressed the button to open the doors of the elevator. When I reached the lobby, Jameron was waiting for me.

He took one look at me before putting his arms around me and pulling me in close to his chest. I heard the beating of his heart quicken under my ear before I started to cry. "Merci. Come here. Please do not cry. Everything will be okay; I will make sure of it. Come, our chariot awaits us."

He kept his arm around me as we walked outside and climbed up into a small quaint bus. "Jameron, I want to go home."

"Hush, we will have our day together, and you can decide after that. I don't want you to leave, Merci."

Ryan

After I helped Merci get back safely to her suite, I went to the hotel. Troy was in Tricia's room, and they were both waiting for an explanation from me. I listened to Tricia tell me about her affair with Troy. Their relationship had started a few months before she became pregnant. She fought with him shortly after she realized she was expecting and that is when she started seducing me. She planned to pass the baby off as mine. It would have worked if Troy hadn't brought Merci to my resort.

"I'm sorry, Ryan. Truly I am, but you always get so anal about your properties. I want more fun out of life than running from hotel to hotel. Troy was there when I needed him to be. Please don't be angry at me; I would like to remain friends."

"Tricia, we were never friends, to begin with. Troy on the other hand was." I turned to face Troy Masters. "I have another question for you, friend. What is it exactly that you have been accusing me of taking from you? I've tried to think of something in our past that I might have done, but nothing comes to mind. You've got my wife, and now I would like to know what else it is that you want from me."

"You still don't get it, do you? I don't want to talk about this in front of Patricia. We will discuss it tomorrow in your office. In the meantime, what do you want to do about our business relationship? I can't continue to work with you anymore, not after what has happened between us."

"You mean after you screwed around with my wife and got caught. If you hadn't found out she was pregnant, would you have continued to pretend that we were friends?"

I turned around and walked away from the two of them and stared out the window. "I do need to give you an honest answer about Merci. I met her not too long ago, and I have fallen in love with her, but our marriage at that time was already over with. I know now that you were already pregnant with Troy's child when Merci and I first met. Tricia, you don't deserve anything from me, but I will be generous just to keep your name and mine out of the paper. I will find another lawyer to represent me. You and Troy can do whatever it is you want to about the child. So that's all there is to tell you."

"Wait one minute, is she the whore who came to our door that night at your hotel? I knew she looked familiar."

"Yes, Merci was the whore who knocked on our door, or rather she was the one who knocked. Merci isn't a whore, and I love her.

Everything about her, and I believe she feels the same way about me too."

Tricia jumped off the bed and rushed me. I felt the sting of her hand across my cheek; then she stood in front of me shaking. "I guess I deserved that, but I only slept with Merci once. How many times did you sleep with my friend, Troy? How many other men did you sleep with besides him? Tricia, I've heard the stories, and I chose to ignore them, so we could make out marriage work."

I backed away from her and looked directly at Troy. "I hope you know what you are getting yourself into. I had my suspicions on more than one occasion for the last few years. I'd ask for a DNA test to make sure that child is yours."

I walked out the door and didn't turn back around. The first thing I needed to do was find another lawyer for both my business dealings and my personal affairs. Then I would make arrangements for Tricia to fly back home.

Merci

I enjoyed being with Jameron; the tour of the city was exciting, and listening to him talk was calming; it was just what I needed. Still, the memory of Ryan's voice saying, *Yes, Merci was the whore*, forced its way into my thoughts all through our afternoon together.

Jameron took my hand and kissed my knuckles. "Merci, please stay with me." Then his face lit up as he smiled at me. "Come, I want to buy you something special. I know just the place that will make you happy. After we shop, I will take you to my favorite cafe to eat."

He led me to a little store in the middle of the street on one side. *De Fun Joy* looked like a bit of a hole in the wall, and unless you already knew it was there, you would miss it. The doorbell chimed as we made our way inside, and the colors and smells in the room assailed my senses all at once.

"Jameron, what a fun little place. This is just the right store to find souvenirs for my family. I love the many bright colors."

A beautiful lighter-skinned black woman entered the room from somewhere in the back. "Jameron Sebastián, why does it tek suh lang inna between your visits? Who dis beautiful gyal yuh bring?"

Jameron took my hand and pulled me close to his side. "Mada, this is Merci Lachance. She is a very good friend of mine."

The beautiful older woman stood there with a blank look on her face, then suddenly her smile lit up the room. "Est ce un spécial?"

Jameron laughed, then kissed the side of my cheek. "She is, and she speaks French. Merci is looking for presents to take back home to her children. Could you help her, Mada?"

I held out my hand to shake hers. "I'm guessing you are this incredible man's mother. It's so nice to meet you; you have a beautiful store here. How long have you been in business, Mrs. Sebastián?"

"Call me, Mada. Jameron, mi like dis one. Cum wid mi, mi ave much to show yuh."

We spent a few hours inside the shop. Jameron's mother was so gracious and helped me find something for my entire family. At the end of our visit, she brought out a beautiful bright blue dress made of a light-weight soft material.

"Try dis on, Merci. Di cola wi bring out de blue of yuh eyes. Cum wi mi. Me wi show yuh weh cya change. Jameron, mek yuhself useful. Wi be right back."

"Mada Sebastián, the dress is beautiful. I can't accept it as a gift from you."

"Jameron tell har it a waah insult to refuse mi gift."

"You heard mi, Mada. Take it, Merci."

"Can you keep it in the back for me. I will think about it." Jameron picked up the sacks of presents that his mother had wrapped up carefully for me to take home to my family. "Thank you so much, Mada Sebastián, I hope to see you again very soon."

I moved away from the woman so that she could hug her son. "Mi hope te see yuh again, Merci."

Ryan

I wanted to do something extra special to let Merci know how sorry I was for making her feel the way I had. My wife was a cheating, whore who had tried to pass off another man's baby on to me. If not for overhearing her and Troy arguing, I might not ever have found out the truth.

"Jameron, I want to know everything about your day with Merci. I can't wait to see her again and tell her my news."

I listened carefully to what Jameron told me. From the way his expression changed when he spoke of her, I knew he had deep feelings for Merci. "So that's all there is to tell you. When I took her on a tour of the city, she fell in love with a blue dress that she tried on in one of the shops in town. She asked the woman to keep it in the back while she decided whether or not she wanted it. I'm sure it will still be there.

"Thank you, Jameron. I will send someone over there to pick it up right away. Are you sure you are okay with this arrangement? I know you care for Merci."

Jameron assured me he would go along with my plans only because he knew things would never transpire between them while Merci still had feelings for me. "Thank you, Jam. And now, I've got another favor to ask of you.

It was easy enough for me to find the dress, and I had a girl in another shop help me find the perfect shoes and accessories to go with it. I would send everything to Merci's suite this afternoon, as well as roses, and the clues to a scavenger hunt that would lead her to me at the end of the evening. Jam had helped me plan every detail of the night out, so it would be spectacular. I hoped it wasn't too late to salvage what we had.

I was more nervous than I could ever remember. As planned, I was sitting on a private yacht waiting for the woman of my dreams to follow the clues that would lead her to me. Jameron would be there along the way to help her. If she chose to accept the challenge, I would see the beautiful girl wearing the blue dress that I had purchased for her at any moment. After that, I planned a trip sailing across the ocean under the St. Lucian sky with a jazz band playing, candlelight, and the sexiest woman alive in my arms to share the incredible night with.

The time ticked by; there was no sign of Merci at all yet. Could something have gone wrong? I reached for my cell phone to call Jameron and make sure things were happening as we had planned just as a heard her melodic voice whisper behind me, "Ryan, I don't know if I can do this again."

I turned around expecting to see her wearing the dress that I sent for her to out on. Instead, she wore a pink tank top and cut off shorts. "Merci, didn't you get the package I sent to you? It should have been there with the first clue to get you…"

"It came, Ryan. I'm sorry, but I can't accept it from you. You've given me so much already. I can't take anymore. I've asked Jameron to take me to the airport. I've got to go back home to my girls. Troy paid for my flight back home. But I couldn't leave without telling you goodbye."

"You can't leave, Merci. We can be together now; it was all a huge mistake; the child wasn't mine after all."

"Ryan, Tricia is still your wife, and you must have been sleeping with her to have the notion that it was your baby, to begin with. After we spent that one magical night together, I went home and filed divorce papers against my husband immediately. My night with you meant so much to me. I never thought we would see each other again, but when we did…well, you know for yourself how badly that night ended for me."

. "Merci, did you read the letter I wrote to you, it explained everything very clearly. I don't love Tricia, not like I love you." I listened closely to everything she was saying to me. This couldn't be happening. No one ever told Ryan West, *No*

"Ryan, I think you are in love with the idea of me. Maybe that's all you were for me too, just a taste of something that was missing from my life."

I couldn't believe what she was saying to me. "Is it Jameron? Did you two sleep together while you were here? Never mind, it doesn't matter?"

"No, Ryan! It's not about him, or Troy, or Tricia! This is about me and the way you made me feel the night we spent together. This is also about the way you made me feel the next time when we didn't, and every time since. You've hurt me worse than my husband ever had. On that first night we spent together, you made me feel like I was sexy and special. But then you took it away from me and made a joke out of it with your wife in the room to witness everything. It took me weeks to stop crying after that night when you left me in the parking lot."

"What can I do to make it up to you now? I want you to stay, please, Merci." I made my way slowly toward her and spanned her tiny waist in my hands. "Give me one night, tonight, and I will make it up to you."

I recognized the yearning in her eyes; it matched how I felt inside. I lifted one of my hands and pushed a lock of hair behind her small ear, then smoothed my thumb up and down her cheek. "Your skin is so soft, and when I do this, the skin on your arm shimmers in the moonlight as the goosebumps come to life. You come to life under my fingers, Merci."

She drew in a shaky breath. "Ryan, you aren't listening to what I'm saying. Yes, you made me feel something that I'd never experienced with a man before, and I may never feel that way again. But you, you Ryan West, caused me more pain than anyone ever has as well. I can't do this anymore. Goodbye, Ryan." She stood up on her tiptoes and pressed her mouth against the side of my lips, then she quickly turned around and walked back from wherever she had come from.

I heard the car door shut; then the final sound of the engine as it drove away from the yacht.

"Mr. West, did you still want me to serve you dinner?"

~~~

Do you want one more book? Please leave a review on your favorite retailer and let me know!

~~

Seaside Sangria recipe by Deborah Lane

Large pitcher.

Cut up, strawberries and blueberries, raspberries, peaches, apple with peel left on, add peach schnapps, and your favorite peach wine or Liebfraumilch and add small bottle seltzer.

Add sugar to taste, crushed ice, and stir!

~~

Bloody Bacon in the Sun Mary

In a large pitcher add the following;

3 Cups V8 juice

The juice from four limes freshly squeezed

Two freshly squeezed lemons

2 Tbsp. Worcestershire sauce

½ tsp. prepared horseradish

2 tsp. tabasco

1 Tsp. old bay seasoning

1 tsp. sugar

¼ tsp. freshly ground black pepper

1 cup vodka

Crushed ice

Garnish with peppered bacon on skewers stuck into celery stalks

~~

Island Mojito

In a large pitcher with crushed ice add the following

2 oz. Rum

2 oz. pineapple flavored rum

2 limes freshly squeezed

2 oz. pineapple juice

2 oz. coconut milk

2 oz. simple syrup

1 oz. Triple sec

Shake then add

9 or 10 crushed mint leaves

Garnish with

Lemon and Lime slices, and

9 or 10 large pineapple chunks on skewers

About the Author:

Robin is married but spent twenty-two years as a single mother of five before she married her current husband. She was a letter carrier for twenty-four years and is now retired from the postal service. She lives in the heat of Arizona where she loves to write her stories and the stories of others.

Robin Rance began writing after a reoccurring dream kept making an appearance. She wakes up regularly with other stories begging to be told. Robin generally writes contemporary romance but also has written other genres including inspirational romance, and a fantasy historical book as well. She finished her first children's book about anti-bullying and has a book of family favorite recipes.

Robin currently has eleven books that have been self-published and is working on releasing five more by next year. She's got a crazy imagination and hopes that you will take a peak and like what you see.

Made in the USA
Columbia, SC
23 December 2017